so why didn't this gi
by news of a dead boo

Interesting indeed.

I heaped three sp...cream as I could fit into the cup without making it overflow then blew on the brew. "You having that spat with Marion means you'll be on the list of suspects." Telling her that I had personally reinforced Chief Conrad's suspicion didn't seem too wise.

She didn't look happy. "You think he's going to question me?"

"Sure as my bunions ache." They did, too. I shifted my weight and slid off my shoes to rub one foot against the other. My chair chose that moment to let out a grievous moan. This woman needed to get herself some real furniture. "No one dethrones Marion's girl, Valorie, without releasing the terrorist inside her momma."

Don't miss out on any of our great mysteries. Contact us at the following address for information on our newest releases and club information:

Heartsong Presents—MYSTERIES! Readers' Service
PO Box 721
Uhrichsville, OH 44683
Web site: www.heartsongmysteries.com

Or for faster action, call 1-740-922-7280.

Murder on the Ol' Bunions

A LaTisha Barnhart Mystery

S. Dionne Moore

HEARTSONG
PRESENTS
MYSTERIES

To Joseph C. M. Griffin, my friend and father. Precious memories, how they linger. . .

Huge thanks to ACFW. Through this organization I learned so much about the craft of writing. Kudos to Penwrights, who helped critique this manuscript. To Michelle Shocklee and Bonnie Calhoun for helping with accuracy, and to Rachel Hauck, Donita Tompkins, and the old ACRW Crit 7, who gave me the ability to believe in myself as a writer and taught me how to fine-tune. Humble thanks to Susan Downs for taking a chance on me, and to her team of editors who got out their polishing cloths to make this manuscript shine. Last, thanks to Sally Black, my very first editor and best friend—you're the greatest!

ISBN 978-1-59789-639-9

Cover Design Kirk DouPonce, DogEared Design
Cover Illustrations: Jody Williams

Our mission is to publish and distribute inspirational products offering exceptional value and biblical encouragement to the masses.

Printed in the U.S.A.

Something about the Out of Time antique store didn't feel quite right that Tuesday afternoon. The rattle of that annoying bell Marion Peters insisted on hanging over the front door combined with the shock of cool air against my hot skin and managed to fry all my circuits and make me feel a little crazy. Kind of like the days when my kids each used to demand all my attention at once.

"Mercy, Marion." I reached up to still the clattering noisemaker and called down the narrow building toward the soda fountain Marion used as a counter at the back of the store. "When you goin' to bless us all by removing this thing?"

No one answered. Strange, that. Silence is not one of Marion's virtues. Come to think of it, her virtue list is pretty short, if you get my meaning. And no one enters Marion's store without her verbally pouncing on them with news of her latest purchase of quality merchandise or her daughter Valorie's most recent show of academic brilliance.

My sweet husband, Hardy, set the bell to rattling all over again as he heaved his plaid pants a little higher and stepped inside the shop and out of the Colorado sunshine. He shot me a grin that sported his pride and joy—his lone front tooth, covered in gold. But the sight of his weathered black face and grizzled gray-black hair has filled my heart with contentment for going on thirty-eight years. 'Course, I don't let him know that too often, or he'd be thinking he's got me wrapped around his little finger.

Hardy shut the door and gazed up at the spastic bell. He reached to silence the thing, fingertips three inches shy of meeting their goal. His cocoa eyes rolled in my direction, waiting. You see, Hardy's as short as I am tall.

I reached up to squelch the bell and patted him on the head, not bothering to hide my smile. "Where'd you disappear to? I looked all around the library for you, then gave up and came here."

Hardy's grin didn't dim. "Went to Payton's to talk music. He tried to sell me a book on playing the banjo."

"You don't play the banjo."

"Yup. Where's Marion?"

"How am I supposed to know? I just got here myself." Reaching around Hardy's slender form, I opened the door wide enough to set the bell to making noise and slammed it hard. We both cocked our ears toward the room for any sound to indicate Marion's arrival.

Hardy guffawed. "Never thought I'd enter a place owned by Marion Peters and not hear her mouth flapping."

I sailed past the old Broadwood concert grand piano that took up one side of the room and peered into one of the two boxes of books I'd purchased earlier in the day. Marion had grudgingly agreed to let me leave the boxes until I could fetch Hardy to haul them for me. "I suppose we can just take this box and go. Wonder where the other one is?" Where was that woman? "Marion!"

"Lot o' wind in them lungs for an old woman."

"You'd better shut your trap, Hardy Barnhart. Years of yelling after you has given me my lung capacity. Marion!"

Hardy's eyes twinkled. "She's giving you the silent treatment. I figure she's still mad at you for——"

"You hush."

"Marion can hold a powerful grudge."

His words came to me through the filter of my own warring thoughts. Something wasn't right. I could feel it. Marion never left the store without flipping the sign from OPEN to CLOSED. And forgetful she's not. Ask anyone who has ever done her wrong. I glanced back at the door. The sign definitely said OPEN.

"You go ahead and load this box into the car. I'm gonna look for the other one."

Hardy shuffled forward. "You paid for them?"

I sent him a healthy dose of the look I made legendary with my children. "Of course."

He held his hands up, palms out. "Just askin'. If LaTisha Barnhart is thinking of starting a life of crime, I want to make sure I get cut in on the loot."

This man. He makes me crazy. I glanced down the length of him and smirked. "Got your drawers hitched too high again, don't you? I can always tell—you start spouting crazy things."

"Yeah, like the day I said, 'I do.' "

"That's not what you said. You said, 'Yes, ma'am.' "

I peeked into the box. The old books, covers frayed

and worn, were neatly stacked, and definitely the ones I'd purchased. I motioned to Hardy, and he lifted the box to his shoulder. I turned and mentally itemized the merchandise in the store. Having worked at Out of Time until my youngest left for college last fall, I knew exactly where everything should be. A few dustless outlines proved recent sales had helped boost Marion's receipts, but other than that, things looked normal. And why shouldn't they be?

The store didn't hold much. A huge oak bookcase, a mahogany secretary, and a cherry dining room set took up most of the twenty-one-foot length. Thanks to her going-out-of-business sale, Marion's overpriced stock now sported tags well within the price range of Maple Gap folk. The store's impending closing had surprised many of the citizens. Everyone figured Marion's elite clientele of wealthy collectors both here in Colorado and across the United States would keep Out of Time a thriving landmark for many years.

So much for that thought.

The scent of old books and dust hung heavy in the air. A draft of cold air raised shiver bumps on my arms. I stilled myself, turned, and studied everything again, forcing deep, calming breaths. Something was eluding me. Whatever stirred my senses to high alert seemed to be strongest at the counter. I returned there and sucked in another breath. And that's when I caught it. A certain strange scent. What was that odor?

A mental image of my grown son at the age of eight bloomed. Tyrone had been helping Hardy build a shed and had sliced his finger a good one on the saw. Tyrone gave out a yelp. I went running. Hardy's dark chocolate face took on a milk chocolate patina at the sight of the blood, so I took charge. As Hardy hit the ground in a faint, I barked instructions to my children on how to care for their father and hustled Tyrone to the car.

I directed our old Buick through town, one hand on the wheel, the other helping Tyrone maintain pressure on the wound. I tell you, blood seeped through that towel faster than I felt comfortable with, filling the air with its copper scent.

That was it! I inhaled the air in Marion's shop, held my breath, and then released it slowly. My stomach clenched hard. Blood.

All my senses flared, spitting warnings, making my head spin. With a hand on the counter, I steadied myself for what I knew needed to be done. As if pulled by an unseen string, I gravitated toward the only corner of the room I hadn't already examined. Some sixth sense screamed at me, telling me to hightail it out of there. But I ignored it, my feet leading the way, my brain screaming at my toes, telling them to cease all forward movement, turn tail, and run.

I focused on the things scattered along the counter, a white envelope, an old-fashioned cash register, brochures of the store, a small bell for service. The now-identified scent of blood saturated the air. My throat clenched. My feet must have finally got the message because they wouldn't move forward at all now, so I steeled myself and leaned forward over the counter.

Marion.

Her head lay in a pool of blood.

Cold shivers tingled along my scalp. My heart skittered. I pressed both hands flat on the counter and squeezed my eyes shut to block the horrible image as shock carried me over the edge of rational thinking into a state of mind where every impulse had its way. I opened my mouth and gave vent.

Hardy came on the run, his steps banging along the wooden floor as he skidded to a halt beside me.

"What's wrong? What happened?"

My tongue stuck to the roof of my dry mouth.

"You getting ready to drop over or something?"

Tears glazed my eyes and turned Hardy into a fuzzy, carnival-mirror image. I raised my hand and shooed him away. "Get back," I finally croaked. "Go back outside. You don't need to see her."

Hardy's eyes got wide. "What you talking about, woman? See who? You ain't been sniffing glue again, have you?"

He sure knew how to get to me, but I wasn't having any of it. "You know I only did that once on a dare. Now you get." I waited for him to retreat; instead, he stared. I flicked my hands at him, hoping he'd trust me on this one. "Hardy. . ." My glance at the place where Marion now rested gave everything away.

Hardy's expression melted into a frown. "What's back there?" He took a step closer.

"No! You'd better not stick your nose over that

counter. I'm warning you. You'll be sorry. Don't look."

"Hardy's coming around, LaTisha." The young doctor of Maple Gap stood in the doorway of Out of Time, divested of its annoying bell at long last by the chief of police himself.

"I think he'll be just fine." Dr. Troy Gordon motioned me to precede him back into the store. "It's not every day one sees a dead body."

I stepped over to the end of the counter, careful to keep my eyes off the form flanked by the police chief and another man I'd never seen before. I gazed down at Hardy's waxy complexion. He needed a thorough chiding, so, being the good wife I am, I warmed to the event like a microwave on high. "I told you not to look. You never do listen."

The doctor knelt next to my man and patted Hardy's shoulder as he tried to sit up. "You'd better lay back down, Mr. Barnhart. You've had quite a shock."

"Naw," he grated out. "She talks to me like that all the time. Ignoring her works best."

My tongue poised to reply, but a wave of dizziness gripped me so hard I felt myself whirling. "I'm a-thinking I'm going to lay me down, too."

Dr. Gordon's wide-eyed face tilted up at me, and he jumped to his feet. Just as my knees gave way, a hand jerked me backward and my body folded onto a chair.

"Head down, LaTisha." Doc's hand pushed my head

between my knees, or as far forward as it could reach over my stomach. Diet *is* a four-letter word, after all.

Within seconds the dizziness began to release its grip. Something tickled down my belly. As my head cleared, I realized the sensation came from my pantyhose beginning a southern migration. Never could get a decent pair anymore.

"How do you feel?"

Doc Gordon's voice penetrated my thoughts. I croaked a little hiccup and raised my head slowly. "I'll be fine." But I wanted air. Real bad. I nodded toward the door. Doc must have understood my silent plea, because he gripped my arm and helped me get up. With his hand directing me, I broke out of that shop and back into the spring sunshine. He helped me get settled into one of the two Windsor chairs he'd dragged from Marion's shop.

"I'll bring Hardy out here, too. I daresay he's had enough excitement in that store."

Within minutes, Doc Gordon returned with a wan, shuffling Hardy.

"You don't look so good," I said as Hardy slumped down next to me and buried his face in his hands.

"Neither did *she*."

I scooted my chair closer to him and squeezed his shoulders, drawing his head down to my chest. "You listen next time I tell you something. Thought you'd done gone and had a heart attack."

I spread my hand across his slender back and wondered how, after thirty-eight years of my cooking, the man had yet to put on more than five pounds. He was too skinny. Of course, he always told me I'd gained enough for both of us.

Hardy's voice came out muffled. "I wouldn't leave you to have all the fun."

The doctor reappeared. "Officer Simpson wants to talk to you, LaTisha. I told him you weren't feeling well and to wait awhile. He's pretty anxious to ask you some questions. Do you feel up to it?"

I twisted around in the chair and saw the young police officer standing in the doorway. I nodded at him, anxious to have the whole incident behind me. "Come on over here and get to your asking."

Doc gave Hardy a pat on the shoulder. "I'll be inside if you need me."

Hardy straightened in his chair as the officer approached. I gave his complexion a good once-over before frowning at the policeman and jabbing a finger toward Hardy. "You can ask me what you need to until he's feeling perky."

"I just have a few questions, ma'am."

"You new to town?"

The young officer swelled up a bit. "Yes, Mrs. Barnhart. I moved into town last week."

I gave the newcomer a good scrub down with my eyes and wondered why I hadn't heard of his arrival. No way was I eager to go through the whole trauma of explaining to this young fellow how I found Marion's body.

"Job doesn't pay well," I started out, making good

and sure he knew I had the upper hand. "We just lost two men a month ago because the city council didn't approve raises. One of them moved his family to Seattle; the other became an insurance salesman."

"Uh, yes, ma'am."

"I'm LaTisha Barnhart. And you?"

"I'm Officer Mac Simpson."

"Not a bad-looking boy. How old are you?"

"Thirty-two."

"Tisha."

Hardy's voice held an edge that I recognized right away. I rolled my eyes his way. "I'm just trying to be neighborly."

"Let the boy do his job."

I huffed back into my chair and crossed my arms, considering. Doesn't hurt to give the new guy a few warnings about small-town living. Who knew? A murder right after a new person arrived in town. . . Suspicious, if you ask me.

With Hardy getting uptight with me, I'd have to summarize my welcome speech. "You must have bought the Hartfords' place. Only house for sale that I know of. I'll bring you some of my fried chicken. Don't want newcomers to feel unwelcome here. I consider it my duty to make sure new people have at least one good square meal. Moving is hard work, and organizing a kitchen takes a woman's touch. You got yourself a woman? Preferably a missus." My eyes slid to his left hand. No ring. "We can take care of that for you, too; just give us a chance."

Satisfied that I'd had my say, I waited for the man

to begin with the questions. He blinked like a barn owl in the sunlight for a full thirty seconds.

"Hurry up and ask what you need to ask. I haven't got all day."

His Adam's apple bobbed, and he cleared his throat. "I—" He glanced at the small notebook in his hand as if it contained the script he should follow. I knew the pages were blank. Noticed it right off. Not much escapes me. Ask any one of my seven children. They'll tell you their momma not only has eyes in the back of her head, but she's got 'em on the sides, too, and the high beams are always on.

Figuring that I had more education about these police things than he probably did, I decided to help him out. "You want to know what I was doing in the store and how I found Marion."

His lips cracked a small smile. "That would be a good start. Yes."

"The chief asked me all this already."

"Yes, ma'am. He wanted me to ask again."

Now if there's one thing I don't like to have to do, it's repeat myself. I tell you once. That's it. You ask for a repeat and you might get it—slowly and with every syllable enunciated—but you ask again, and I'll call the ear doctor and set up a fitting for you to get yourself a hearing aid.

I leaned forward, deciding I'd give this boy a second chance. This time. Since he was new and all. "I went into the store to pick up some things I bought earlier. Hardy came in after me. Something seemed funny when Marion didn't start talking right off. That's Marion for you. She never had any need for quiet. Anyways, I went around the counter and there she was." I had to push hard at the sight of her that flashed in my brain. Forcing back my emotions, I went on. "Payton heard me—that's the owner of the music store next door, don't suppose you've met him yet—and he came over right after Hardy fainted. He's the one who called you boys. That's it."

Officer Simpson scribbled in his book. "Did you see anything suspicious? Hear anything out of the ordinary?"

"I smelled blood." And still did. I swallowed hard. "Took me awhile to figure out what that smell was, but I did. That's when I thought to look behind the counter."

Voices carried over from the doorway of the shop. The chief of police and a man I didn't recognize talked for a minute before the stranger went back inside. Chief Chad Conrad caught my gaze and headed our way.

Simpson saw his boss coming. His expression became severe. "I must say you're pretty calm for someone who just saw a dead body."

I latched onto his eyeballs with mine. "Look here, I've had seven children—five of those are boys. Between bumps, scrapes, and breaks, there isn't much more that'll shock this momma. If one of them boys didn't drop blood every day, they'd thought they was girls. You feelin' me?"

"Uh, I—" Officer Simpson's face became a fiery red, and he gave his boss a mortified look. "Why, *no*,

Mrs. Barnhart, I'd never—"

"That's not to say I'm not sorry for Marion. She was a pillar in this community, but she's also a woman who is well known for her high-handed ways and churlishness. I figure most folk wanted to give her a good push at some point or other, but that doesn't mean I did it!"

Chief Conrad presented a slick authority figure beside his younger counterpart. He also maintained the honor of Maple Gap's most eligible bachelor, though Officer Simpson's hand, sans ring, might mean the chief's days retaining that honor were numbered.

The chief leaned to whisper in Officer Simpson's ear. Relief flooded the younger man's face. He sent me one last, almost terrified glance and went back inside.

Conrad hooked his thumbs over the edge of his thick black belt. Squint creases on each side of his eyes, coupled with his thin lips and dark widow's peak, gave him the look of a tough guy. "I should appoint you to the force, LaTisha. The way you intimidate people is amazing. You and I could do the good cop/bad cop routine quite well."

Hardy snorted to life. "Yeah, but you're a little too mean looking to be the nice guy, Chief."

The two laughed themselves stupid at that. I crossed my arms and glared. But the idea of being a cop, an investigator, or an officer on the force. . .

"I've only got one more semester before I'll have my degree in police science," I offered, pointing a finger after the departing Officer Simpson. "Bet that boy doesn't have one of those."

"I can't be too choosy at this point, LaTisha. The budget restraints are stretching us as it is." His gaze shifted to the store, and I could almost hear his brain churning.

He doesn't know how he's going to manage a murder investigation as short staffed as he is.

Conrad pulled his gaze from the store. "How are you two feeling?"

I glanced at Hardy, relieved to see the familiar sparkle in his eyes.

"We'll survive."

Couldn't help but wince at Hardy's choice of words. Chief just grinned.

My curiosity got the best of me. "How do you think it happened?"

"We won't be sure for a while. State police are on their way with a mobile crime lab vehicle. Could be she just had a bad fall and slammed her head against that radiator."

"She'd have to have fallen awful hard. It's not like she weighs a lot."

Conrad pursed his lips. "True. We'll let the state men do their thing to find out. In the meantime, there are a few more things I need to ask you. Payton has offered us the use of his store while Nelson finishes taking pictures of the bo—"

I shook my head and ran a finger across my neck so he wouldn't shake up Hardy again with reminders of Marion's body.

"—uh, the details."

"Does Hardy need to stay?" If Conrad insisted on talking bodies and blood, my man needed to leave or we'd be sweeping him up in a dustpan after he shattered.

"How about I talk to you first. While we're talking, if Hardy could play us a tune. . . ?"

Hardy pushed to his feet. "Sure thing, as long as Payton doesn't try to sell me any more banjo books." He laced his fingers together and stretched them, palms out in front of him, until his knuckles cracked. "I'm a piano man."

Payton O'Mahney needed no introduction. His store décor said it all. Walls swirled red and green with vertical stripes of blue. Purple carpet. It all screamed at you as soon as you opened the door and stepped across the threshold of his music store, Offbeat. Never did understand what the boy hoped to express with such bold patterns. Oh, right, his sense of style. Uh-huh. That was it.

Two grand pianos sprawled along the sides, and a row of four uprights lined the wall adjacent to the antique store.

Payton strutted into view from the back of the store with a wide smile stretched across his face. He was sporting a new look. Last week he matched his walls. This week he had apparently gone to the other extreme with monochromatic white. Even his hair was a dull pearl. He wore sharp-pleated white pants with rolled-up cuffs and a linen vest over a stark white shirt. He looked like he'd stepped off the page of a coloring book. If I'd had some crayons, I would have gladly done the honors of coloring inside the lines.

Hardy cocked his head one way then the other, a puzzled expression drawing his brows together as he followed Chief Conrad into the store. "Am I senile, or did you move things around since I was in here this mornin'?"

I didn't miss the way the chief perked up at this observation and narrowed his eyes to study Payton's reaction.

Payton's smile didn't waver. He tugged a handkerchief from his back pocket and dabbed at his upper lip. "Swapped those uprights with my sheet music and CD display. Looks better this way. Quite a job, though." He motioned toward the grand. "The grand hasn't moved. Go to it, man."

Hardy needed no further invitation. He gravitated to the nine-foot concert Grotrian like my knit skirt clings to my pantyhose. Speaking of which—I frowned down at the unflattering outline of my legs. Static cling. I peeled the material away, disgusted when it returned to mold around my thighs all over again. I'd have to get some lotion and rub it on my legs. If I didn't have all these males looking, I'd spit on my hands and rub them over my hose. That'd take care of the problem. For a while, anyhow.

Payton hopped closer and extended his hand to me as if he'd never met me before in his life. I smacked his hand away. "You knows me, boy. What's wrong with you?"

Without missing a beat, Payton spun away and grabbed Chief Conrad's hand, cranking it up and down. "You can use my store for as long as you need, Chief. I'll walk down to the corner and get some donuts and coffee if you'd like."

Chief's look of disdain as he disengaged his hand was quickly replaced with what could only be his stern,

I'm-on-duty expression. "That won't be necessary, Payton. Thank you, though. I just wanted to talk to LaTisha and Hardy somewhere out of the way of the coroner."

I kept a close eye on Payton. He seemed jumpier than normal.

A loud bass chord shattered the peaceful silence as Hardy began his attack on the keyboard. I recognized Chopin as he began to weave a spell of sound around us all. Even Chief Conrad stopped to admire my man's skill. Hardy's hands ran up and down the keyboard with a nimbleness that belied his gray hair.

When Hardy got nervous or upset, the piano was where you would find him. If the rather fragile upright at our house didn't fit his emotional liking, he would traipse down to this place and play either the Grotrian or the Mason & Hamlin. One of these days I planned on buying him a baby grand, but it would have to wait until our two youngest finished college. Not to mention my finishing my own degree.

"And to think he's never had a lesson in his life." Chief motioned me to take a seat on the sofa while he sank into the nearby armchair. The nice thick cushion felt like heaven after the hard Windsor. And speaking of things hard. . .

"Who's going to break the news to Valorie?"

Chief Conrad stroked his jaw. "Why, I suppose I am."

"She acts tough, but she's really a sensitive little thing."

"I'll remember that." He flipped open a small notebook and pulled a stubby pencil from his breast pocket. "Now you told me earlier that you returned to the shop to pick up some books you had paid for this morning."

"I told Marion I'd bring Hardy back to help me lug the books out of there. After lunch, I headed over to Marion's, Hardy in tow, but we detoured to the library. Hardy must have got lost in the place, because I didn't see him until we met up at the antique store. He told me later he'd left the library and come here to visit Payton."

Conrad glanced over at Payton, who had positioned himself halfway between the sitting area and Hardy. Payton nodded his affirmation. The chief scribbled something and directed another question my way. "How was Marion this morning? Anything about her behavior seem unusual?"

"She was on the phone. Talked on the thing the entire time I was there. All I got out of her was a nod when I handed her my money, and a grunt when I asked about picking up the boxes later."

Chief frowned at his notebook. "Did you hear anything or see anyone?"

It was on the tip of my tongue to say no, but I slowed down to ponder the question. In the background, Hardy spat out a series of short staccato notes and slid into a song with a definite blues undertone. One of the songs he had composed. Something about the music tickled at my brain. An impression. I couldn't get it to reveal itself fully.

I narrowed my eyes and focused on Hardy's hands,

hoping to force the thought into focus, but I could only recall that sickening, permeating scent of blood. "I can't think of anything, Chief."

"Did you by chance notice something out of place on the counter?"

And why would he be asking that unless it was important? I did recall a flash of white. Rectangular. An envelope or something. I decided to reverse the table, so to speak, to see if he'd drop a little more info for me. "Was it big?"

Conrad's right eye squinted as his lips curved slightly. "You tell me."

Beans! The man wasn't going to give anything away if he didn't have to. "I think I remember glimpsing a flash of white as I stood at the counter. An envelope, I think."

He nodded and jotted something down in his notebook.

"All right. Let me talk to Payton and Hardy, and I'll get back to you. Someone's got to know something. One of the officers mentioned hearing a rumor about a feud between Marion and Dana Letzburg, Valorie's teacher. Do you know anything about that?"

Did I! "I was at Regina's the other day and overheard Dana complaining to her that Valorie didn't deserve to graduate after what she'd done."

Conrad raised his eyebrows. "That's it? That's all you know?"

" 'Course not. I asked Dana about it as we left, and she said she'd caught Valorie cheating. Had evidence, too. Marion hit the roof and accused Dana of having it out for her daughter."

He bounced a steady tempo against his chin with the end of his pencil. "Interesting. Anyone else you know who had a problem with Marion?"

"Sure. Half the town. Regina gives her a bad haircut every chance she gets."

"Excuse me?"

"You know, Regina Rogane. The hairdresser. She declares that Marion gets to talking and debating, and it makes her so mad that she always manages to mess up her haircut. Then there's that new guy in town, Mark Hamm—something strange there, for sure. Whenever Valorie would float into the shop saying she'd gone to his restaurant to eat, Marion's lips would get tighter than a clam. She sure didn't like the news."

"Hmm. You think. . . ?"

"Never know nowadays."

I leaned forward, motioned him to come closer, and lowered my voice. "Payton's another one to keep an eye on. You know the row he's started about this building. Marion wanted to sell to some contractors, and Payton kept pushing it to be declared a historical site. When I worked here, they were always arguing back and forth over something. And he was always late on his rent. Drove Marion crazy."

One last note lingered in the air; Hardy's dramatic ending punctuated what I'd just shared with Conrad. Hardy lifted his hands from the keyboard as Payton broke into applause. Chief and I joined in as Hardy slid off the bench and crossed over to us.

Chief gripped Hardy's hand hard, then relaxed back into his chair and tucked the pencil behind his ear. I knew another question was on its way. "If I might ask, what made you quit working for Marion?"

Hardy fell onto the sofa beside me with a loud laugh. "Oh, she didn't quit, Officer Conrad. Marion fired her. Made Tisha madder than a hooked fish."

Would you hurry yourself up?" I glared at Hardy, who hung three steps behind as I hustled from Payton's music store on Spender Avenue, past Out of Time, to the hotel on the corner where Spender intersected with Gold Street.

"I've not got your zest, woman. Would have driven the car around here if you'd have let me." He mopped his face with a bright red handkerchief, stuffed it into his back pocket, and raised his chin. He looked like a banty rooster ready to crow. "Mmm. The smells coming from Mark's place are mighty tempting."

As if the man didn't know every day of the week the smell of good cooking.

Mark Hamm, owner of Your Goose Is Cooked, managed to draw more customers off the streets because of the fragrant air his restaurant produced than because of the quality of the food. I knew this to be true—I'd eaten there.

But food is not what had me hauling Hardy toward the restaurant. I wanted him to do some investigating for me while I went to another section of town. I had no patience to sit and wait until the state police did their tests to figure if Marion's death was an accident or not. Falling against a radiator would put a hurting on someone, sure, but kill them? Nah. My gut told me Marion's death was no accident. Questioning those residents of our fair town whom Marion had penciled in her little black book would give me a jump start on the chief.

I lifted my head to catch the scents wafting across the street from the restaurant. "Smells an awful lot like fried chicken. You have any money on you?"

Hardy slipped a thin wallet from his pocket, unfolded it, and held it open for my perusal.

"Three dollars?"

He glanced down into the wallet. "Living with you makes me a poor man. I saw you snitch my ten out yesterday."

"Only because of *your* overdue library books."

Hardy folded his wallet. "Where's the change?"

I glanced right, then left, making sure no one was looking in our direction, and patted my chest. "Between the two of us, we've got nine dollars and some change," I assured him. "I'll give you the five and you go eat at Mark's. Ask him some questions about Marion and Valorie."

Hardy stared at me from under his bushy brows. "I'm not the nosy one. If I go there to eat, I'm gonna eat, not talk."

"Was you who suggested to the chief I had a motive for murdering Marion. The least you can do is help to clear my name."

Hardy's brows drew together, a thoughtful look in his eyes. "Don't know. Being married to a murderer. . . They arrest you and you move to the pen, I'll have room for that Grotrian."

"How you gonna pay for that thing?"

"How else? Write a book on the torture I endured being married to a cold-blooded murderer. Probably even get a movie made about me." His eyes shifted down the street toward Marion's store, where Chief Conrad stood talking to the coroner. "Maybe I'll just hitch myself down there and have a little talk with our man in blue."

As he started off in that direction, I latched onto the back of his collar and yanked hard. "Unless you want to be the main event at the next funeral, you'd better get your skinny self back here."

"See? I'm threatened with bodily harm every day."

"If you hadn't shot off your mouth to the chief about Marion firing me, I wouldn't need you to do this."

"She did fire you."

How could this man be so thick? "No. I quit."

Hardy crossed his arms, his lower lip pushed out in his classic look of pure mulishness. "Only after she fired you."

"And you saw how fast Conrad jumped on that. Like a man with a pimple, he was going to squeeze and squeeze until he got something."

"Well, if you didn't do it, what are you worried about?"

"I'm not worried!"

He raised an eyebrow. "Then why are you yelling?"

"I'm not—" My jaw snapped shut when I noticed the two patrons outside of Your Goose Is Cooked, picking their teeth and staring my way. Good town folk. I waved at them and beamed a huge smile. "What's the special today, boys? Smells like fried chicken."

Wilbur Gates rubbed his ample stomach. "All you can eat."

"Sounds good to me," I trilled over at Hardy. "What about you, honey-babe?"

"Sure, dumplin'," Hardy drawled. "Whatever you want."

Wilbur and company moved off down the sidewalk as Hardy and I crossed the road arm in arm, acting fine and dandy.

I stopped at the door to the restaurant and took another quick glance up and down Gold Street to make sure no one else would be privy to my words. "You get yourself in there and do that askin' before they put a ball and chain around my ankle. You'll starve to death without me." Before he could reply, I plunged my hand down the front of my dress and rooted around for my small stash of cash.

Hardy flashed his gold tooth.

I glowered and passed him the five-dollar bill.

"I know I'm gonna regret asking this, but what do you do with the coins?"

"Don't you worry your head about it. You just go on in and get busy. I've got some investigating of my own to do. I'll meet you back at the house."

"I'm sure not making any promises," he said.

"You'd better. And bring the car home so it doesn't sit in front of the library all night."

Hardy wasn't even listening. Didn't take him long

to move himself when food was to be had.

After retracing my steps back to the crime scene, I crossed to the other side of the road and passed the elementary school, made a left onto Foster Court, and came to a halt opposite the combination post office and gas station. Two houses down, Dana Letzburg's Victorian home sprawled on a spring green lawn.

Marion's phone conversation that morning had involved someone else. Apparently Chief Conrad hadn't thought to ask me if I knew whom that other person might be. . . .

I slid off my shoes, rubbed one aching foot over the other, rearranged the seam of my hose across my toes, and slipped back into the low-heeled pumps. This murder stuff was killing my bunions.

Generations of Letzburgs had lived in the old two-story. Town legend marked Dana's great-grandfather as the sheriff during the crazy days of the gold rush when Maple Gap raised itself from the dust. When an assayer decided to steal the miners' gold, Maple Gap almost became a ghost town, but citizens did their best to keep the men from leaving. A few townspeople pooled their money and ran an ad in some East Coast papers, inviting women to come to the little town, marry, and settle down.

Some of Maple Gap's old-timers still vowed that the assayer's stash of gold had yet to be found.

One summer, after my children got wind of the legend, they dedicated the rest of their vacation to searching for it, digging holes wherever they went. I spent the summer sending Hardy out to fill those holes and offer apologies to our rather irate neighbors.

The memory of my babies, now grown and gone, settled like a melancholy lump in my stomach as I hobbled up the short flight of steps to Dana's front door and rang the doorbell.

Soft footsteps on hardwood, a flash of color through the glass sidelight, and the door swung open to reveal Dana. Her smile welcomed me before her words. "What a surprise, Mrs. Barnhart. I was just grading papers."

"I thought we might sit and talk a spell."

Dana opened the door wider and stepped back. "Come on in."

I gave the gal a once-over. "Regina did a good job on your hair." Indeed she had. Dana's short dark hair sported muted highlights I hadn't really noticed when I'd asked her about the allegations against Valorie Peters.

My hostess made a face. "All Regina's talk of politics drives me a little crazy. She should run for office, as passionate as she is about things happening in this town."

"She was on a committee with Marion a few years ago."

"They probably disagreed on everything," Dana said. "I'll make us a pot of tea."

Tea. Oh no. The vile brew makes me burp. I

almost suggested a tall glass of water in lieu of the tea, but Dana was out of sight. I huffed and decided I'd just toss it back and gulp real quick. That way I wouldn't taste a thing.

I shut the door and studied the mess in the living room on my left. Anyone would guess the young woman either had just moved in or was preparing to move out. Boxes of every size covered the living room floor. One comfy armchair and a floor lamp seemed the only pieces of usable furniture.

"Looks like you've still got your work cut out for you." I raised my voice to be heard.

A splash of water measured Dana's progress on tea preparation. She appeared in the doorway that separated the kitchen from the dining room.

"I keep trying to get rid of boxes, but it seems they multiply while I'm sleeping."

"It takes more than a week or two to get truly settled, no matter where you move." Stepping into the living room, I gasped as the rest of the room became visible. "Hardy'd throw a shoe if he saw this."

This turned out to be a polished ebony concert grand.

I trailed my fingers down the slick length of the piano, admiring every inch of the beauty, until I could see the maker's name. Steinway. I was awestruck.

Dana flicked on the overhead light and straightened a stack of papers on the cushion of the armchair. "Hardy is welcome to come play anytime. Teaching doesn't allow me much extra practice time, but I play when I can."

I ran my finger over the silky, cool surface of the instrument. "My man would worship at your feet for a chance to play a Steinway. What model?"

"D." She stopped beside me and played a little tune, then made a face. "Payton tuned it last week. I walked over during lunch to let him in. Got back just in time for my next class." She waved a hand at the keyboard. "I haven't tried it yet."

I spread my fingers over the keys and played a C scale, the extent of my piano-playing knowledge. As the sound resonated through the room, I raised my brows at Dana.

Her lips formed a straight line. "It, uh, doesn't sound too good, does it?"

"He tunes our upright. If you're not happy, make that boy come back and do it again."

A low-pitched whistle signaled the impending doom of my happy tummy. Dana straightened and hurried off toward the kitchen.

Left behind, I decided to snoop. My eyes skimmed over the bookshelves beside the piano. Classics mostly, but some of the books looked to be leftover from Dana's days in college. By the look of things, most of the books were still in boxes.

I went over to the armchair, glanced up to make sure Dana was out of sight, and gave the papers on the cushion a cursory glance. Looked like papers on diagramming sentences or some equally horrid grammatical nightmare. On the table holding the lamp were the remains of a half-eaten cookie and a book with a tattered-edged paper marking the place.

I leaned over to get a better view of the book. *Days of Reckless Gold.* The ruffled piece of paper acting as bookmark appeared as old as the book. Interesting.

Maybe it was a letter from her great-grandfather. I glanced over my shoulder to make sure I was alone before I riffled through Dana's personal items. "That tea almost ready, honey?"

"Almost," Dana called back.

Satisfied, I snatched up the book. It fell open to reveal the bookmark as an old letter.

"I like my tea with honey and sugar," I called out, trying to keep conversation going so I would know Dana's location.

"I've got both."

I zoom-scanned that thing as fast as I could, noting a name—Jackson Hughes—and the signature; the first name was so scrawled I couldn't make it out, but the last I could. Letzburg. Probably Dana's relative. Interesting.

I slowed down enough to read each word. Dana's great-grandfather, the sheriff, had the diary of the old assayer, Jackson Hughes, and it held a scribbled drawing. Now that'd be worth something to those interested in the history of Maple Gap.

I wanted to read further, but when I heard the rattle of teacups, I knew my time was almost up.

"Tea's ready, LaTisha."

With great care, I refolded the letter and closed the book, returning it to its original position on the table. A nudge here, a push there. When I turned, Dana stood in the dining room doorway, her smile frozen in place.

4

My brain was smoking trying to come up with an excuse good enough to explain why my backside stuck up in the air and my nose hovered over Dana's end table. I pointed at the papers on the chair, shook my head, and groaned. "Mm. Wish you'd been here to help my youngest with sentence diagrammin'. Lela took longer than any of the others to catch on."

Saved my bacon from getting fried in her grease. But how much of my little story about diagramming sentences did she believe? Probably not much.

Shrugging it off, I took note of Dana's decorating style as I followed her through the dining room toward the kitchen. Lace curtains, lace tablecloth, lots of knickknacks in the china cabinet—it seemed to be the only room with nary a box.

The kitchen, too, appeared fully operational. Lace everywhere—the window, the table, even hanging over the edge of the glass-fronted cabinets. The side door also had a thick, heavy lace valance covering almost the entire window. Made me itch to think about it. A silver service sat proudly on top of a table the size of a large pizza. What scared me most, though, were the dainty wire and wood kitchen chairs. I conjured an image of my broad base—if you get my meaning—overflowing that little chair until the wire bent and snapped, leaving it nothing but a coil of wire and kindling.

But Dana didn't seem to have the least doubt her furniture would be safe. "Have a seat. You're my first guest since I moved back."

With great concentration, I lowered myself into that chair, alert to the slightest protest from the frail structure. It held solid beneath me, and I sighed my relief, though my hose betrayed my earlier tugs and began to roll again.

But it was time to get down to *real* business. "You see the police at Out of Time on your way home from the school?" Though she taught English to the seniors, the school across from the antique store was kindergarten through twelfth grade since Maple Gap wasn't very big.

Her reaction to my question interested me greatly. She didn't meet my eyes, gasp in shock, or show even a speck of curiosity. She continued the process of adding water to the silver teapot as if her entire life hinged on the completion of that task.

She flicked the lid closed and wiped the side of the pot dry. Now, either this lady knew something I didn't, or she was one of those types who takes great pride in her ability not to show emotion at shocking news. She didn't seem the latter type. Something in this girl's brain was clicking around, and I aimed to figure out what it might be.

"It's a small town." She gave me a tight smile. "I stopped at the corner to fill up my car. Tom mentioned seeing you, Hardy, and Payton with the police. I didn't ask for details. Was Payton robbed?"

Maybe she didn't know, then. So I tried for shock value. "Nope. I found Marion laying dead in her shop."

Dana settled the teapot on the table. "That's too bad." She met my gaze, eyes wide.

I searched her expression, satisfied that what I saw didn't appear to be genuine surprise. By her own admission, she hadn't asked for details from Parker, the gas station attendant. So why didn't this girl seem the least bit flustered by news of a dead body? Interesting indeed.

I heaped three spoonfuls of sugar and as much cream as I could fit into the cup without making it overflow then blew on the brew. "You having that spat with Marion means you'll be on the list of suspects." Telling her that I had personally reinforced Chief Conrad's suspicion didn't seem too wise.

She didn't look happy. "You think he's going to question me?"

"Sure as my bunions ache." They did, too. I shifted my weight and slid off my shoes to rub one foot against the other. My chair chose that moment to let out a grievous moan. This woman needed to get herself some real furniture. "No one dethrones Marion's girl, Valorie, without releasing the terrorist inside her momma."

"Everything I told Marion about Valorie's cheating in class is true. I have evidence."

"Don't matter none. You've been here six months. Only long enough to begin the school year. People won't trust you yet."

Her eyes widened in disbelief. "But I was born and raised here. I taught Valorie when she was in my third-grade class."

"Yeah, and you left for the city. Deep down, Maple Gapites don't like city folk much. Townsfolk'll think it strange to have our first murder in over a hundred years after a new person arrives in town."

"Mac Simpson's been here less time than I have," Dana pointed out.

"But not long enough to know Marion or be on her bad side."

Dana must have forgotten the intricacies of small-town life since her escape ten years ago. Despite the gal's claim to the town as her legacy from her great-grandfather, everyone in Maple Gap knew Dana had nothing but city blood in her veins now. Tainted blood. You could see it in her hands. City girl hands—soft hands with big blue veins that popped out like earthworms holding their breath.

I lifted the teacup, tested the temperature—lukewarm—raised the cup in salute, and slammed back the contents in one gulp. My belch drew a scowl of disgust from Dana.

"This here little murder is a serious thing. Towns-people don't like to think they're going to have to lock their doors at night. Don't suppose such a thing sways you, though, being from the big city and all, but here it's gonna be in the headlines for weeks. Mark my words."

"If the police are looking for people with a beef against Marion, they'll have a very long list."

"Yup."

For a girl suspected of murder, she seemed pretty calm. On the other hand, I was a suspect, too, thanks to Hardy. Difference was, I knew I didn't do it.

Dana lifted the teapot and twitched it at me, asking me without words if I wanted a refill. I didn't. But the conversation needed to continue so I could squeeze out the information I needed. With my stomach already churning more protests, I held out my teacup and pasted on my best smile as she poured. "I was in the shop this morning when you and Marion were talking on the phone."

Dana slid the sugar bowl closer to me. "*Marion* called *me*."

"Didn't sound like a friendly conversation."

"She wanted me to drop the whole thing with Valorie. You know how badly she wanted her to get into Stanford." Dana's jaw firmed. "But I can't let Valorie get away with cheating. What if she's been doing it all along? What if her valedictorian status is a sham? It would really hurt her if I let this slide. Marion didn't understand that."

Right on. I agreed wholeheartedly. "What was the whole thing about a book?"

She lifted her teacup and took a long sip. Her cup clattered onto the saucer. "A diary. It's not a big deal, but I should have known better than to ask about it."

"What diary?"

Dana blew a wisp of hair off her forehead. The brown strand fluttered upward and clung. "Instead of unpacking every box, I decided to leave some things stored. The attic is full of stuff, so I was trying to weed out and make a storage area. I sorted through some old books and donated some to the library. The rest I thought might bring a good price from collectors, so I asked Marion to sell them on consignment. She wouldn't do it, said it was against her policy, but she agreed to buy them from me."

I laced my fingers and digested that tidbit. Marion always took things on consignment, unless she had changed her policy since I quit. Doubtful. The woman hated change, but she sure delighted in finding ways to nettle people she didn't like. "Go ahead."

"Marion gave me a fair price, so we were both pretty happy. Later I noticed an old diary was missing that I'd wanted to keep—uh, a relative of mine wrote it. I kept meaning to ask Marion about it. Then this thing with Valorie happened. Long story short, when I did ask—"

"That's what she was saying to you this morning."

"She told me if I didn't drop the thing with Valorie, I could kiss that diary good-bye."

"Did she find it?"

Dana scraped her chair back and stood up. "I guess I'll never know now."

I bumped my chair away from the table, understanding the silent dismissal. "You take to heart what I've been telling you. The police will come knocking any minute." That's when the craziest notion rattled through my brain. You see, the previous Sunday at church, I had seen Dana come into service by herself. Officer Mac Simpson had been there, too, holding the door for her. Later on I had caught him scooting over to offer her a place to sit. Dana had appeared to take his attention in stride, but who knew?

"Better stay clear of Officer Simpson. Won't do you any good for people to be thinking he's sweet on you, you being a suspect and all. Might make people think you went in together on murdering poor Marion."

5

No car in the driveway meant Hardy hadn't returned home yet. Where could that man be? I couldn't wait to get at those books in the backseat of the car. The school needed the donations desperately. That's when it hit me. Boxes. Plural. In all the excitement, I never did find that second box. I would have to make sure Chief Conrad knew it was my property. Maybe he would let me in to look for it at some point.

Our old four-bedroom, clapboard-sided house enfolded me in unnatural quiet when I entered. Our youngest daughter, Lela, had left for college last fall, leaving the house quiet. Too quiet. Years of the constant drone of little voices whining and teenagers fighting—or was that the other way around?—made coming home now a depressing routine.

I flipped on the hall light and deposited my keys on the semicircular hall table. The silence struck a discordant note that made my heart hurt. But before I could warm myself in the shawl of memories, a steady tickle around my waist made me frown hard. Not again. I grabbed the elastic of my hose and hiked up the steps to our bedroom.

There, I let go of the waist and pushed out my stomach. The elastic creeped downward and curled like an ocean wave over my belly. When it stopped midway down my stomach, I worked the hose slowly downward, over the tender chafed skin of my thighs, then tugged them free. Sweet liberation! Soft bedroom slippers completed the transformation to comfort, and I imagined my bunions singing the "Hallelujah Chorus."

I scanned the room. Hadn't changed the bedspread or painted the room in close to twelve years. The walls appeared more mustard than lemon yellow, and the bedspread sported broken threads. A nice blue would be a welcome change of color. That would make a fun project for Lela, Shayna, and me when the girls came home for Easter holiday. The boys would probably gather for a basketball game with their father.

The goodness of life swelled within me as I surveyed the walls again with new excitement. White walls would work, too. A Wedgwood-patterned border would bring class to the room. Our solid oak furniture had served us well and remained in great shape, except for that chunk taken out of the nightstand when Hardy, busy trying to hang brackets for a shelf in the room next door, had forgotten to take off his drill bit extension and. . .

That's when I finally noticed the red light blinking on the answering machine. I leaned forward to press the PLAY button.

Hi, Momma.

The voice of my youngest, Lela.

Just got in from a late class and wanted to tell you I can't come home during Easter vacation. There's some algebra I need help with, and the tutor is willing to work through the holiday with me. It's free, too, so I can't pass this up. I'll miss you, Momma. Tell Pop to stay out of trouble.

She wasn't coming home for the holiday.

My eyes locked on the bevy of pictures on the dresser across the room as the answering machine beeped its conclusion. Two wedding pictures—Tyrone and Cora, Bryton and Fredlynn. Seven high school graduations—all seven of my babies. Four college—Tyrone, Bryton, Shakespeare, and Shayna. Lela's picture would be there in three and a half more years. Caleb, our youngest son, would graduate this year.

Mine would be there soon, too. Hardy had encouraged me to fulfill my dream and get my degree. Dear, dear man. His selflessness made it possible, scholarships made it feasible, and my job at Marion's had covered the rest. Until I'd quit. . . Been fired. . . Whatever.

But even the fulfillment of my dream didn't cover the throb of my disappointment. Lela wouldn't be home for the holiday. For the first time I could remember, not all of my babies would share the Easter holiday with Hardy and me. I forced the disappointment away. After all, the others would be here, plus Cora and Fredlynn, so that would make eight. Still. . .

My eyes drifted to the pictures again, and the burn of tears threatened. But I had no time for all that. My latest college assignment needed to be completed before tomorrow morning, when I would meet with my virtual professor and classmates. An essay on the intricacies of photographing a murder scene. And what good timing.

The textbook would tell me what I needed to know, sure, but. . .

Chief Conrad's photographer would be the best source. Other than the newly hired Mac Simpson, "Tank" Nelson was the only officer employed by Maple Gap, and he had been a photography enthusiast for years.

On my walk back from Dana's, the presence of two state police cars and yellow crime scene ribbon let me know that the state police had arrived from Denver. One of the uniformed men had been taking pictures, Tank Nelson at his side.

I gave a little bounce on the mattress, which helped jettison me to my feet. Starting the paper wouldn't be a problem—just get me in my kitchen. I worked best there. Plucking up my books and papers, I made myself a good cup of mocha and settled at the sturdy oak dining table to sip and compose an introductory paragraph.

I scratched out a rough paragraph, rolling the words through my mind as I rose to cook. My best thinking happens when I cook. Dragging out a huge pot, I began mentally checking off the list of ingredients needed for a good, hearty stew. I chopped vegetables then jotted a few notes for my paper and wrote a couple of paragraphs. Next break, I pressure-cooked chicken while I mixed and rolled dumplings, then wrote for an hour as the stew and chicken and dumplings simmered.

The tantalizing smells energized me, and the words formed in my mind. I gulped my cooled mocha and visualized the photographer taking pictures from every angle of Marion's body. The height of the camera, aperture, weather conditions—everything needed to be documented. My essay became a mini crime scene on paper.

Finally, I set my pen aside and read over the report. It read well with a few corrections, but all that work had given me a powerful hankering for pecan cake with caramel icing, so I left the essay and mixed together the ingredients. Within thirty minutes, I was sliding two round cake pans into the oven.

I reviewed the day's events. The shock of seeing Marion's body, crumpled and broken, became superimposed over the images of my days working as her employee. My eyes burned, and grief began to take small nibbles from my spirit. Marion might not have been overly kind or easy to get along with, always shoving inventory lists and packing slips into my hands, wanting me to read them to her because she'd forgotten her glasses again. But we'd shared a few laughs, and in our own way, we'd respected each other. I expect most felt that way about her.

Hmm. One person didn't.

Dana hadn't appeared shaken by the news.

Make that two people.

Payton.

I made a mental note to try to figure out what Chief had meant by saying he wanted to question Payton *again*. I knew for sure he'd only questioned Hardy and me at the scene of the crime.

Maybe Payton's anxiety stemmed from the idea

that Chief might wonder why he and Marion fought so much. Most of the time, truth be told. Either Marion was barking at Payton for being late on his rent payment, or he was nagging her not to sell the shop, reiterating its importance as a piece of Maple Gap's history. But Chief's pointed look at Payton when Hardy observed out loud that Payton had rearranged the pieces in his shop got me to wondering.

I got up and tugged a package of cornmeal from the pantry and began preparing corn bread to accompany the simmering stew. As I mixed in an egg, my mind churned over Marion's conversation with Dana. The young gal seemed a strange mix. She caught a student red-handed in the middle of cheating but didn't flinch when the mother of that student turned up dead. I'd give anything to know what Chief Conrad thought of the possibility of Dana doing the dreaded deed.

And that letter bothered me, too. Dana's great-grandfather's letter would be a prized possession in light of his status as town legend, just as the house that had always belonged to the Letzburgs would remain a comfort to future descendants. I'd have to ask Mark Hamm if he knew anything about the Letzburgs or the assayer, Jackson Hughes. Since he wrote articles on the history of the town for Maple Gap's paper, he must know some of the details of the legend.

I slid the cake pans over and made room for the corn bread, then lifted the lid of the dumplings and inhaled the rich scent. Comfort food. I closed my eyes and inhaled, imagining the sounds of doors slamming and childish laughter. "What's for dinner, Momma?"

Where had the time gone?

I whipped up enough piecrust for three pies, spooned cherry filling into two and blueberry into one, topped them with another crust, and sprinkled sugar and cinnamon on top. I pulled out the pecan cakes and slid the pies in. The corn bread needed a bit longer, so I adjusted the oven racks to accomodate the extra load, then put together the caramel frosting as I waited for the corn bread to finish and the pecan cakes to cool.

As a young mother, I'd thought the children being gone would be a relief. Now my mind reeled backward to the days of trying to keep up with the raging appetites of the growing boys. The memory made me laugh out loud. If I could bottle the smell in the kitchen at this moment and send it to them, there would be five grown men standing on the front porch, drooling.

With an ache, I realized I'd made all their favorites. From cherry pie to corn bread and caramel-pecan cake. Lela favored the chicken and dumplings. I hoped no one else canceled for Easter supper.

After stirring the stew, I replaced the lid and adjusted the heat. The timer on the oven went off. I snatched up the pot holders, rescued the corn bread, then plopped a dab more softened butter into the frosting being stirred by the stand mixer.

Hardy chose that moment to enter the side door beside the stove. He came to an abrupt halt as he stared at the dishes in the sink and the food in various stages of preparation.

"You cookin' for the funeral already?"

I pointed my spatula at a chair. "Doin' schoolwork; now sit and eat."

"I'm not hungry." He dragged a chair out and sat. "Mark's fried chicken is almost as good as yours."

I glanced at the wall clock, its face a picture of all our children. A Christmas gift from son number five. I quickly looked away from the beloved faces and glanced outside the kitchen window. Pinks and oranges streaked the western sky. "You're late."

"Had a tune running through my head, so I hopped over to Payton's to run my fingers through it."

"You've been there a long time."

"Payton had closed the store." Hardy hopped up and lifted a lid. A cloud of steam rose from the pot of beef stew. "He let me in, though."

"I think that boy still grieves over losing his last chance to play professionally."

"Yeah. His hand's been bugging him a lot lately, too."

"Maybe he should have it looked at again."

"Too much money. He'd like it, but the shop doesn't make him rich. I told him he needed to stop scooting those pianos around by himself. That metal sheet music display made a mess of the hardwood floors."

"He should try flipping a rug over and sliding the piano around on that."

Hardy rolled his eyes. "Too late now." He scrunched up his face and looked at the calendar on the refrigerator. "When is he scheduled to tune our upright? It sure is needin' it."

"Said he couldn't get to it until Friday."

Hardy jerked his head back and made a face. "What'd you say? He got a call from Dana and practically ran me out of the store so he could go tune her piano. Didn't know she even had one."

"A Steinway, Model D. She offered to let you play it." It was my turn to be puzzled. Odd that the boy would run to do Dana's tuning and then tell us we had to wait almost a week. "You think he's sweet on her?"

"Payton? Naw. He loves himself too much. Maybe they're gonna compare notes about Marion's death."

That made me rub my forehead. My brain was on overload with all the cooking and fretting and essaying I'd been doing. But Payton and Dana comparing notes? Maybe I'd find out something more if I hauled Hardy over there to play the Steinway. "I'll make sure to get you over there."

I began to feel the exhaustion creeping up my body and released a tired sigh. I cast a glance over the food, then at the clock on the wall, feeling Hardy's eyes on me.

I turned off the mixer and took out the pies, then busied myself with the dirty dishes. "Did you ask Mark those questions like I told you?"

"Nope."

"What you mean, 'Nope'? You want me to go to jail?"

"Tisha."

There it was. That tone. Whenever Hardy calls me Tisha, I know he's onto my game. I gripped the spatula tighter and scraped down the sides of the bowl.

"Why don't you come sit yourself down while you frost this naked cake?"

I didn't dare look at him. "You just want to lick the bowl."

"No," he said, his voice low. "I want to knows what's got you cooking enough for our entire family when it ain't but the two of us. You knew I'd come home stuffed with chicken."

That made me bite my lip and ponder an answer. "I came home to an empty house." There. I said it.

"You missing our babies?"

That did it. The faucets started flowing, and I turned my head away. Hardy's chair scraped along the floor, then I felt the warmth of his body behind me. His arms slipped around my waist—well, as far around as they could reach. He laid his head against my back and squeezed me tight as I started to drip tears onto the counter.

"They're making their way, sugar," he whispered. "It's what you raised them to do. Lela'll be home during spring break."

"No."

His head lifted. "What you mean, 'No'?"

"When I got home," I said, dabbing my eyes with a green-striped dish towel, "Lela'd left a message. She's struggling with math, so she's getting a tutor and working over the holiday."

Hardy's hand on my back massaged in little circles. "It's all right, Tisha. Some of them are still coming over.

I'll get them all to help me cook up a huge meal, and we'll deliver it straight to you there in jail."

I should have known! I snatched that dish towel off my shoulder and whipped it around into a tight, lethal twist as I rounded on Hardy. He flashed his insufferable grin and leaped away as I let go with the damp towel. He managed to dodge my first snap, but, lightning quick, I wound the towel again and finally landed a slap along his wrist.

He howled.

"Serves you right, tormenting me."

He rubbed his arm and collapsed in the chair, laughing. The man needed to be taught a lesson.

"You went into that restaurant and stuffed yourself silly and didn't even bother trying to help me find the culprit, and now you're talking about me going to jail!" I nailed him with my eyes. "What you smiling at?"

"You didn't let me finish. I didn't have to ask any questions. Valorie came into the restaurant while I was biting into my first chicken leg."

I lowered my brows at him in warning and picked up the frosting. "You'd best be telling me everything."

With that, I settled myself in the chair opposite and scraped up a big glob of the frosting to begin dressing the cake.

When Hardy didn't continue, I raised my eyes to see him looking with longing at the frosting. A tinge of guilt at the blow I'd landed made me soften. Pushing to my feet, I got a big serving spoon out of the utensil drawer and scooped up a spoonful. His eyes lit up, reminding me of the days when the children would wait in line as I baked for a taste of my homemade caramel frosting.

"No more," I told him as I handed over the spoon. "I've got to have enough to cover the cake with. Now talk."

He took a good lick of the icing. "Valorie looked upset. Over what, I don't know, because she didn't know about her momma yet. Tammy, that waitress you like so well, she and Valorie whispered; then Tammy disappeared and Mark came out."

He gulped down another bite and wiped his mouth on the back of his hand. "I'll take your cooking over Mark's any day."

Now how can I be sore for long with such sweet talk?

Ever since Mark Hamm opened his restaurant over two years ago, the man kept mostly to himself. When I worked at Out of Time, on the occasions when Valorie would drop in to see her mother, she would talk about Mark, and Marion would grow sullen. I rolled the situation around in my mind.

The spoon was almost clean of frosting, and Hardy didn't look too inclined to come up for air, so I prompted him. "What did Mark do?"

"He gave her a huge hug."

"Was it a fatherly hug? A boyfriend type of hug?"

One last lick and he plunked down the spoon. "Boyfriend!"

"Those things happen all the time. She *is* eighteen," I reminded him.

"It seemed just a friendly hug." A definite twinkle lit his eyes. "You know, like I'd give Leslie Monroe."

A young college friend Shayna had brought home years back. A pretty gal. "You keep talking like that, and she'll be spoon-feeding you in intensive care. Now don't get off subject—tell me what happened next."

"Nothing. Mark sat down across from her, and they began talking so low I couldn't hear a word they said."

I smoothed the frosting into amber ripples, disappointed Hardy hadn't learned more.

He held out his empty spoon. I raised my hand to smack the spoon away when a slow smile spread over his lips. I knew that smile.

"You'd better not mess with me, boy. What you hiding?" I leaned back in the chair and slid open the utensil drawer to fetch a clean spoon. The chair hit the floor with a thwack, and I scooped up more frosting and surrendered it to Hardy.

"Didn't learn nothing else from Mark and Valorie. But then Chief Conrad came into the restaurant. He sat down and talked to Valorie for a good long while. Must have been telling her the news. She started really crying."

"Well, of course. It's not every day a girl finds out her momma's been murdered."

Hardy took another lick. "Yeah, but Mark went right over to her and gave her another one of them hugs. I'm thinking the chief was a little shocked by it, too."

"What did he say?"

"Say? Nothing. He left."

Morning light assaulted my eyelids no matter which way I flopped in bed. Surrendering to the silent call, I sat up and stretched, renewed, reinvigorated, and ready to go. Hardy snored on, proof he was living and breathing. Aggravated at his ability to sleep so soundly, I jiggled the bed. He twitched, smacked his lips together, and rolled over. I heaved a sigh and decided to let him sleep. At least until I finished my morning online college course. Then I'd rouse his old bones with the smells of bacon and ham.

After Lela moved out, I had wasted no time converting her room into an office, maybe to erase the melancholy of her leaving. Now my computer and books graced the desk, and the walls soothed with a sage green, hiding Lela's beloved periwinkle. But memories clung like wallpaper. The times when, as a little girl, Lela had pestered her brothers and sister into playing hide-and-seek. And Lela, always thinking she had them outsmarted, would choose her favorite spot to hide. In her closet. No matter how many times we tried to explain to her she needed to use another place, Lela went back to the closet.

Such memories never failed to bring the burn to my throat. I even went so far as to open the closet door and imagine her bright, joyful brown eyes staring up at me. She'd make a mad dash for home base, knowing all along she would be caught and tickled.

My, how things change. I sucked in a deep breath and shut the closet door on its current mess of school material, printer paper, and books.

Switching on the computer and establishing a connection, I forced away the melancholy and began the process of typing and uploading my essay. For the first few minutes after signing on, I chatted with my classmates, sentences popping up on the screen full force until the professor entered the virtual classroom for our Wednesday morning class.

He reviewed information from the last class— aperture, weather conditions, shutter speed—and began a comparison of the differences between photographing a crime scene and everyday picture taking. He ended by announcing the next assignment.

Pushing up from the cushy office chair, I returned to our room to shower and get ready for the day. Along the hallway, the pictures of my babies at various stages of their life weighted my every step. The entire time I showered and dressed, I wrestled with putting what could no longer be into its proper place. I had grandbabies to look forward to, and with seven children, I expected a busload. That thought alone served to lighten my steps.

Pulling the door to our room to within a crack, I headed downstairs, my stomach already rumbling at the thought of cinnamon toast. Made my mouth water when I added bacon and ham, oatmeal, a side of grits, and a passel of eggs to the menu. Cholesterol city. But

I'm dying a happy woman.

Sure enough, the combined smells made it under the crack of our bedroom door, because Hardy shuffled into the kitchen blinking and grinning just as I placed a platter of eggs on the table.

"You come on and eat. These eggs won't be good cold." I gestured to the seat, my heart warmed by the sight of Hardy, tousled and toasty from bed. Made me wish I could crawl back in. All this walking and talking trying to prove my innocence was wearing me out.

Hardy settled himself and tugged the platter of scrambled eggs closer to his plate. I jerked back a chair and plopped down. He didn't waste any time. "Lord, bless this food. Let it slide down real good and do what it needs to keep us going for Your glory. Amen."

"Positively irreverent."

He cocked his head at me. "Ear-what?"

"Never mind."

He shoveled some of the eggs onto his plate. "I think I'm going to work on that garden this morning. It's time to get my tomatoes started in the greenhouse."

I concentrated on cutting my ham into small bites and stabbed four chunks onto the fork. "You'd better put a rein on them plans. I've got more investigating to do, and I need your help. Chief asked me if I knew anything about something white on the counter at Marion's shop. It must be important, and I aim to find out what it was. You can be a second pair of ears for me."

"But if I don't get those tomatoes started, I won't get as many tomatoes."

"Mmm-hmm." More than likely he was more worried that fewer tomatoes translated to fewer jars of his favorite salsa come summertime. "It's the first of March; you've got a few days."

Hardy frowned so hard his eyebrows drew down at the edges. "It won't take me long."

"It won't, because you're gonna help *me*. You can worry about your plants tomorrow."

He toyed with his eggs a bit before he popped a generous forkful into his mouth. He chewed quietly, swallowed, blew on his coffee, sipped, and chomped on a strip of bacon with his good front tooth and lots of gum-work.

I stirred my oatmeal and tried to conjure up a real good reason for denying him his tomato planting. His head bowed over his plate as his elbow bent and lifted, guiding the fork to his mouth. He sure loved my salsa, and I loved him loving my cooking.

I shoved away my half-eaten oatmeal and pointed at the dish in the center of the table. The lone piece of bacon sent my mouth to watering anew. "You eat that last piece so it won't sit on my hips all day."

Obediently, he reached for the slice and tore off a piece, chasing it with a bite of eggs. He raised soulful eyes at me. Cocoa brown with flecks of gold and long lashes that every one of our babies inherited. I can tell you, my heart melted into a puddle right then and there.

Something gave down deep inside. I tried to shore up my crumbling determination, but Hardy looked so disappointed. I heaved a breath and crossed my arms, trying hard to look stern, as if my heart wasn't already mush. "All right, then, but you'd best hurry. I want to be out of here in an hour."

He upended his coffee mug and slapped it back down on the table, tooth shining. "You a good woman, Tisha. A good woman."

"Maybe they'll give me time off for good behavior."

He guffawed and pushed his plate away. "As long as you'll have time to make that salsa before they put you in the can." He smacked his lips together. "Can taste it now."

"It's probably indigestion. You ate so fast, it's all a blur in your belly."

Hardy's answering grin showed his unconcern. He got up and ambled over to tuck his feet into his ratty sneakers, lined up in a neat row beside his Sunday shoes and everyday loafers. "Then leave me your recipe and I'll figure it out for myself. You wouldn't want me to starve while you're eating gruel."

He ducked the spoonful of egg I shot at his head and slammed the door behind him so hard the glass rattled.

Egg slimed a path down the door and plopped onto the floor.

Maple Gap's police station hailed back to its early days as a booming gold rush town. But just as the town took off, the gold trickled out. Two-thirds of a narrow, two-story brick building, with a false front, housed the police station. The other third of the building held the offices of a local attorney.

Scared me silly to think I might be seeing more of the inside of that police house than I wanted. I shut the car door and imagined it sounded much like the door of a jail cell. Hardy's declaration had left Chief Conrad frothing at the mouth. That, coupled with me being the one who found the body, spelled indictment if I couldn't find the real criminal.

"It ain't gonna happen, and you know it," Hardy piped up as he slid out of the car. "You're making too much of this, LaTisha." He came over to stand beside me, a knowing frown on his face. "Your fingerprints aren't anywhere in that shop except those books you bought. They's looking for someone with a motive. Someone who has a real problem with Marion."

True. True. "And Chief really isn't looking at anything right now since he doesn't have the results back from the state police." At least, I hoped that was the case. It really *could* have been an accident. I doubted it. Just couldn't seem to shake the feeling that she didn't simply fall. But Hardy was right. No sense in letting my imagination run wild when we both knew I was innocent. Such thoughts would only serve to waste my mental energies.

Confidence renewed, I followed Hardy up the steps. He held the door as I glided into the station and bestowed my best smile on the young officer at the desk. Officer Mac Simpson.

When he caught sight of me, his eyes widened

and—did I imagine it?—he turned pale.

"Good morning," I trilled, trying to inject every grain of sugar I could into my voice. "Officer Simpson. I was wondering if I could have a word with the chief. I need to ask him about getting a box from Marion's shop."

"Only he can answer that, and he's not in right now." His words came fast and furious. He grabbed a pen and began to scribble madly. "I'll write down your request and put it on his desk."

I braced a hand on the rather cluttered desk and leaned forward. "Then I guess I'll tell you my second reason for dropping by. You might have heard that I'm pursuing a degree in police science. Our professor has us studying police photography procedures, and I wanted to know if Officer Nelson could give me some tips. We're real good friends, you know. Go way, way back. He played ball with my oldest, begging a meal at my back door every chance he could."

Simpson cleared his throat and reared back in his chair. The chair dipped hard, and he flailed his hands out to catch himself.

I smothered a laugh and tried to appear concerned. "Oh, honey, you be careful. I had me one of them chairs before. Downright hazardous, they are."

His face flamed red as he released the edge of his desk and tilted the chair forward until his feet hit the ground. He cleared his throat, a sound much like the grinding of a truck's gears, and his tone grew hard. "I can't do that, Mrs. Barnhart."

"Could you at least call him and ask? I've got a paper due soon, and I would really like to talk to an expert."

"I'm sorry."

I dared not show my frustration. Simpson wouldn't budge, and I couldn't blame him a bit. Still.

Hardy'd been quiet. I cast a glance his way. He had nested on the wooden bench beside the snack and cola machine, his neck craning as he looked over the selections like a man starved.

"You just ate."

He raised his eyebrows at me. "A man can look."

I gazed at the door that led to the back offices and wondered if I should yank it open and sing out for Nelson. That's when I got an idea. I faced Simpson. "What's Officer Nelson's extension?"

His brows lowered, and he crossed his arms.

I stepped over to the pay phone on the wall by the vending machines and dug around in the waistband of my skirt for the coins I kept coiled in the elastic of my hose when I wasn't wearing something with pockets. I got a dial tone and punched in the numbers for the police office. The phone rang on Simpson's desk. He scowled at me. I grinned. He picked up the phone and returned it to the cradle, cutting off my call. With a grunt, he picked up the receiver again, punched in a number, and growled something I couldn't quite understand.

Within thirty seconds, Officer Nelson came through the door grinning from ear to ear. "Mrs. Barnhart! How's that Tyrone doing? He a daddy yet?"

"Not yet."

"What can I do for you?"

"I saw you helping out the state police taking pictures of Marion. You know I'm getting my degree in police science—"

"Good for you!"

"I wondered if I could ask you a few questions about photographing victims for a paper I'm writing. It's due soon." Never one to forget the way to a man's heart, I added, "I'll even send over the pie I made just last night."

"Why, sure. Can't beat that as a bribe." His laugh was hearty as he held the door open. "I'll even be a good boy and share with Simpson and the chief."

I tried my best not to smirk when I nodded over at Officer Simpson.

He didn't look up.

I shifted my attention to Hardy. "You stay put. I'll be back."

Hardy plucked up a tattered old magazine with a beautiful celebrity on the front. His smile went huge. "You go ahead. I think I can find something to keep me entertained."

"Be careful—you might have a heart attack." With that, I spun on my heel and lumbered along after Officer Nelson.

Officer Nelson snapped his camera onto the tripod in front of him. "I use a tripod since my hands don't normally give me a steady shot. But until yesterday, I've never photographed an actual body." Blond wisps formed a comb-over that did nothing for his overall appearance. One could easily see that Thomas "Tank" Nelson had earned his high school nickname for good reason.

His small office held little in the way of furniture and smelled of chemicals and bad coffee.

An ugly feeling that I just might be listening to the details of photography all day if I didn't try to lead the conversation in the proper direction made me break out in a sweat. Had to be a way to finagle things around to the questions I *really* needed answered. "Awful dark behind that counter at Marion's—did you have trouble fixing the lighting?"

"I used my flash as backlighting. Since my automatic settings compromised my depth of field, I decided to use manual mode."

Feigning interest in this information, I squinted one eye shut and peered through the viewfinder, knowing my next words would be a gamble. "How do you adjust for objects that are light in color? Like that white paper on the counter at Marion's shop."

He crouched to take my place looking through the viewfinder of his camera. "Shiny objects prove a problem, as do white. Marion's jewelry caused glints, as did the service bell on her counter. The white envelope full of mon—" Nelson's head snapped up; his eyes skidded in my direction.

I regrouped quickly. Better for me to ease up and play the innocent. Hands on hips, I jerked my head back and fixed him with my best don't-mess-with-me expression. "What you lookin' at me like that for? You surprised I know so much? I know all about the problems caused by shiny and white objects when photographing scenes. Between Marion's silver bell thingie on the counter, the envelope, and all those bracelets she wears, I figured you got some hands-on experience with how to temper glare and probably some great advice from the state trooper."

My pounding heart slowed as the glint of suspicion seeped from Nelson's eyes. His shoulders relaxed. "You're right. Photographing shiny objects can be difficult. Contrary to what you think, I haven't had much experience with such things." One side of his mouth rose in a smile. "Usually when I photograph a scene, it's after the thief has taken the jewelry."

I punctuated his statement with a little laugh.

"But watching Officer Lawton taught me a few things about technique."

Now, unless I wanted a verbal rendition of Officer Lawton's tips, I needed to cut this visit short. Chances were Tank would not be supplying me with any further information—on the crime scene anyhow.

I slowly backpedaled toward the door, showing as much interest as I could in the processes Officer Lawton had gone through to photograph Marion's body. When Tank paused in his recital, I used the excuse that Hardy was waiting and extricated myself from his office, thanking him for his time. Tank insisted on escorting me back to the door leading to the front of the station, spouting more details of his technique with flash, until I felt I could produce my own pop of white light.

I thanked him again and pushed through the door. I stopped dead in my tracks. Straight in front of me, Hardy's rear end poked up from where he knelt on the hardwood floor.

"What you doin' with your tail stuck up in the air?"

Hardy shot to his feet and pointed to the floor. "I lost my money."

I studied the wide planks of the old wood floor. A mental image of Hardy spilling his change and watching it rattle along and slip between the cracks made me wonder how many hundreds of dollars in coins might rest below the old floor. In all these years, could be enough collected under there to at least buy Officer Simpson a decent chair.

I glanced over at the young man. He appeared oblivious to Hardy's distress, engrossed in paperwork of some sort. My brain latched onto the seedling of an idea. Paperwork. . .envelope. . . "Mon—" could have been money. It was worth a try.

I crossed my arms and settled my eyes on my man.

He retreated, hands raised, palms out. "You're up to something."

I winked and raised my voice for the benefit of Officer Mac Simpson's ears. "You lost your money again? What am I gonna do with you, man?"

Mac lifted his head, his face hardly concealing his aggravation. Touchy, touchy.

I jabbed a finger at the young officer, and his eyes widened. "Any money been turned in to you today?"

Mac cringed as I sauntered closer. "No, ma'am.

None today."

"Hardy misplaced some yesterday, too." At the desk, I shifted my weight forward, hands braced on the edge of the desk, until my eyes came level with his. "You know anything about that?"

He ran a finger around his collar. "Uh, we found a substantial amount yesterday."

I turned back to a slack-jawed Hardy. "You lose it at Marion's?" Before he could answer, I signaled with another wink. "When I checked your wallet, you only had that five." I leveled my gaze back on Simpson. "You find any at Marion's?"

"It's a crime scene. We, uh—we found a substantial amount. . ."

"In a white envelope?"

Mac Simpson's head bobbed then stilled. His lips tightened. "Why don't I let you talk to the chief about it when he returns?"

Not a chance. "You said a substantial amount?"

"Yes, ma'am."

I swung back to Hardy, elated over what Mac had just spilled. I clamped down hard on my excitement and continued my charade. "How much were you missing? Ten dollars, wasn't it? Can't be ours, then."

"No." Hardy frowned. "It's not ours."

Before Officer Simpson could form a reply, I shooed Hardy out the door of the police station. Mission accomplished.

7

Maple Gap's weekly paper, the *Distant Echo*, waited on the porch. Hardy handed it over without a word. Probably still miffed over the flap at the station.

"I told the truth." I'd made the same statement three times on our way home. I hated his silence, knowing after thirty-eight years what it meant.

I saw the flash of white from his eyes before he went through the door and straight upstairs. My chest locked down tight on my heart. Surely he didn't think I'd gone too far.

Opening the refrigerator, I yanked out the pot of beef stew and put it on the stove to heat. As always, the flavors would be better today after mingling overnight. I broke off a corner of corn bread for me and one for Hardy—if he would eat with me. If he didn't, fine. Let him be that way.

I dug around in the utensil drawer for a couple of spoons, trying to reassure myself. I'd made sure to suggest just enough to lure Officer Simpson into spilling the information I needed. Didn't Hardy want me to clear my name? It was his fault I was in this mess anyhow.

I flicked off my shoes and rubbed at my feet. The stew would warm up fast, filling the kitchen with its rich, beefy scent. If Hardy wanted to eat, his nose knew the way.

As I picked up the newspaper, flyers slipped out

and spread their glossy sheen over the table. The paper's headlines proved intriguing and predictable, many of the articles centered around Marion's murder. Old Michael, editor of the paper, must have rushed to get the articles in before the paper went to print. A picture of the front of the store, cordoned off with yellow crime scene tape, graced the first page. A small story to the right of the lead documented Dana's accusation, along with a short interview with Valorie, who confessed the cheating allegations as truth and leaked to the public the fact that her mother had not been happy with her.

I wondered if that knowledge made her a suspect in Chief's mind. I knew what it made me think.

Another article recapped the ongoing struggle between Payton O'Mahney's fight to block Marion's sale of their building by having it declared a historic site. The city council would hear the citizen arguments for and against the proposal on Thursday evening before they voted.

I scoured this article, surprised to find that Mark Hamm, who became a member of the council after a longtime resident died six months before reelection, planned to recuse his vote. Strange. What reason would he have to do that? I mulled this over as I retrieved my bowl of stew.

Most council members recused their vote when a conflict of interest prevented them from voting legally. Perhaps there was a connection between Mark Hamm and Marion's building? Could his relationship with Valorie have some bearing on his decision to forgo voting on the matter? And if Marion had already been upset with Valorie over her visits to Mark's restaurant, would her daughter's cheating send her over the edge?

I turned the page and found an interview with Chief Conrad in regard to his first murder/homicide as police chief.

So. . .he did think it was more than an accident. I wasn't surprised, of course, given Marion's disagreeable nature.

The article continued by reporting that Conrad acknowledged there were certain persons of interest, but the tests run by the state police forensics team would shed further light and help clear a path to arrest if there had been foul play. "The innocent have nothing to fear from my investigation," the reporter quoted Conrad.

Last of all, I skimmed over Mark Hamm's most recent column on historical tidbits he'd discovered as an amateur historian. Every other week he had something new to share about the gold-mining days of Colorado. Sometimes he slipped in a commentary on current events. I marked the article with a pen so I'd remember to read it later.

I stirred the stew, releasing a puff of fragrant steam, and took a bite. Needed a little more pepper. Hardy's vacant chair brought me back to my domestic dilemma. Where was that man? This was getting serious. Making me fidgety to the point that I lost my appetite halfway through the bowl of stew.

I dumped the dishes into the sink and set about

packaging the remainder of the food from my cook-a-thon the previous evening. I broke the stew down into small portions more suitable for the two of us and began to stack the bags in the freezer.

The phone chirped. I wiped my hands and waited to see if Hardy would answer. On the third ring, I gave up on him and plucked the cordless from its base.

"Hello."

I welcomed the baritone of our oldest son, but my enthusiasm sprung a leak when he started right off with the reason for his call.

"What d' ya mean you can't come home?" Not another cancellation. I gripped the phone tighter. "Cora's been working every day, traveling all that way without a problem, but you don't think she can make a three-hour drive here?" Frustration rose in my chest. I cleared my throat into the phone.

"It's the doctor's orders, Momma. Cora's getting close to her date, and he wants her to start taking it easy. I'm even cutting back my hours to be home with her."

From deep down inside, the voice of reason scraped its finger across my mind. I squeezed my eyes shut. It was best this way. Really. I should be thrilled that my son and daughter-in-law would be so willing not to risk Cora's health, or the baby's. My first grandchild. Grandchild. This equaled old. Washed up. Life over. Gone to seed.

My children don't need me anymore. They're capable.

"I know you're disappointed, Momma. But just remember you'll have your first grandbaby soon."

I nodded against the phone, dried the lone trail of a tear, and fought to keep my voice steady. "Tell Cora we love her and to take care of my grandbaby."

With a vicious stab, I punched the OFF button, grateful for the solid counter to support my weight as my legs became quivery and my vision blurred. I should be understanding. Forgiving and kind and unwilling to be angry about Tyrone and Cora's absence from Easter supper. And if I kept saying those things to myself long enough, the hurt might bleed away.

I don't want all my chicks back in the nest, Lord, but they could at least come by to cluck at me once in a while.

My eyes landed on the bowl of stew I'd heated for Hardy. It was time for him to eat, and he never turned down the notion of food. Unless he was mad at me. "Hardy!" I yelled at the top of my lungs. "You'd better come eat, or I'm gonna eat it for you." I listened hard for a reply, satisfied to hear the scuffle of feet on the floor above.

"You'd better keep your lips off my food. I'll be down in a minute."

In a jiff, I'd reheated the stew and set his place at the table, all the while fretting over my dwindling list of Easter supper guests. I snapped the seals closed on the remaining food storage bags full of chicken and dumplings and stacked them in the freezer, the blast of cold air doing nothing to cool my rising anger. At my children. At my husband. At myself for being so cranky when I'm so blessed.

When the dining chair creaked behind me and I

heard the clink of the spoon against the bowl, I didn't turn. Let Hardy be the first one to speak. I'd had enough.

"The newspaper sure has a lot to say about Marion," he offered. "Did you see the police beat about the theft?"

My mind snapped to attention. Now how'd I miss that juicy tidbit? Drat it all, and just when I had taken a vow of silence. Now he had the paper. I gulped down my pride, though it nearly choked me to do so. "Read it to me."

"Not much to read. It just says the police were called to 35 Rolling Way on Monday evening—that's Dana's house, isn't it?—in regard to a reported book theft."

Book? Who would miss a book unless they placed great value on it? Could it be the diary she'd accused Marion of taking? Why did the diary mean that much to her?

My last dumpling slipped from the pot into a crock. Chief and I needed to talk. He could confirm if it was about Dana's diary or not.

Keeping my hands busy always helped me focus, and this news needed to be analyzed. Could explain why Payton seemed so shook up at the chief's presence. Maybe since Payton had been at Dana's tuning the piano, he had been questioned over Dana's stolen book previous to Marion's murder. Hmm.

I wanted so badly to know Hardy's thoughts. I risked a peek in his direction as I wiped the countertop. His eyes darted left to right, the paper spread out before him, spoon firmly clenched in his hand. Beyond sharing what he read in the paper, he would remain silent about the episode at the police station, knowing his silence pricked at me. After all this time I'd been married to the contrary man, his tricks were nothing new to me. Even worse—they worked.

Finally, he folded the paper and set it aside. He didn't look my way one time.

I heaved a sigh of resignation. "You're thinkin' I went overboard today, aren't you?"

He peered at me from under his bushy brows. "You could get that boy in trouble if you're not careful. Tricking him into revealing things. . .and you weren't right being less than honest."

My hackles were rising in self-defense. "But you did misplace money."

"You took it out of my wallet. Said so yourself, and I'm not arguing the point with you, Tisha. He's a young man on the police force trying to make his way in life. If he were one of yours, you'd squash anyone who tried to put him in a bad light." Hardy scraped the inside of his bowl clean and pushed it forward. His brown eyes speared me. "You stop giving that boy a hard time."

I turned my back, knowing he was right, and pressed my lips together. My hand grabbed for a long knife to begin the process of slicing the pies. I wasn't quite ready to be humble. I'd let a slice of pie be my peace offering. Nice, sweet cherry pie. I covered it in whipped cream and slid it before him.

Our eyes met. He understood the symbol of my silent plea for forgiveness.

"Who called?" he asked as he picked up the fork.

"Tyrone. They can't come for Easter."

"Too bad. But I figure she needs to be careful since this is her last month. You remember how careful you were when you were carrying Tyrone?"

How could I forget? My stomach was so huge with baby I thought for sure I would pop before I gave birth.

"You couldn't get off the sofa that one day and had to get on the floor and crawl to a chair."

The memory brought a smile to my lips. I tore off a piece of plastic wrap to cover the pie. "And you did nothing but laugh at me when I told you."

"Yeah." He rubbed the side of his head. "You cuffed me a good one for that. Come to think of it, you always got mean the month before your due date. Seven times." He lifted his fork and paused. His gaze met mine, spilling over me like warm brown gravy. My throat swelled almost shut, and I reached out a hand to trace a finger down the side of his face.

Hardy was right: I'd been tough on Mac Simpson. Officer Nelson, too, but I decided I wouldn't tell him about that one. A woman has her pride.

As he forked in another mouthful, he flipped the paper over. "Says here someone posted a reward for information on anything suspicious in regards to Marion's death."

"A reward?" I'd missed that, too! "How much?"

"A thousand."

"Woo-wee." I pulled down an old picnic basket and

placed the pies and a crock full of dumplings inside. "I'm going to take these dumplings over to Valorie's house and see how she's doin'. Then I'm going to drop off these two pies for the boys at the police station. You coming?"

"Naw." He stretched and scratched his chest. "I need to get caught up on my beauty sleep." A slow smile of approval spread across his face.

Just as it was for him, he knew the extra pie was my peace offering to Officer Simpson. Of course, Simpson would think I was just being nice. I smothered a smile. Who knew? Maybe it would loosen his tongue and grant me some more juicy tidbits.

"As if you didn't sleep like a dead man last night. The only way I know you was alive was the snoring." Hefting the load, I stuck out my hand. "Give me the keys to the car and I'll be out of here."

Hardy dug around in his front pocket and dropped the keys into my hand. "If Old Lou breaks down, call the garage. I'll be sleeping."

8

"Old Lou" referred to the beige Buick we'd bought on Tyrone's tenth birthday. The car was as familiar to me as my kitchen. A spot of blood on the backseat from Tyrone's almost-severed finger, stains from baby Shayna getting carsick a few hundred times, and the smell of old leather. Though Hardy kept the car running, its purr had deteriorated to a congested cough over the years. Still, Lou kept going and neither of us saw any reason to replace a car whose longest trip ended up being the few times we ventured into Denver or Colorado Springs or went to visit the children.

I plunked the basket into the backseat and started to slide behind the wheel but got stuck. You'd think after all these years of living with a full-figured woman, he'd remember to slide the seat back for me. Not him. I backed my body out, pulled the lever, and slid the seat all the way back, then shimmied behind the steering wheel. I let go a huge sigh of relief to be off my feet.

At my age—and my motto is don't ask, don't tell—I refused to wear the orthopedic granny shoes I saw on the feet of other older women. You can bet my bunions chastise me daily for the abuse. As sorry as it sounds, wearing stylish shoes—sans comfort—is my one point of great pride.

Okay, two.

Dressing to the nines and sailing down the aisle of

our church in one of my lovely hats is another weakness. That's where that rich young ruler got himself in such hot water. If he'd have thought twice about where his decision would take him, he'd have been willing to shake off his pride and give up his wealth. So, see, I'm safe. I can take off my hats anytime and be as humble as the next person.

Lou chugged me past Sasha Blightman's boutique. I craned my neck to see the robin's egg blue Scala Downbrim hat perched on the head of a mannequin. Every hair on my head stood on end with envy. I'd eyeballed this little piece of divine creation ever since Sasha placed it there, and I was happy to know that she hadn't sold it during her sidewalk sale over the weekend.

Sasha's slender form, easily recognizable in the elegant lime green pantsuit, rearranged the jacket on one of the mannequins in the store window. I couldn't help myself. I slowed Old Lou down to get a better glimpse of that hat. Sasha waved when she glanced up. Maybe if I got that reward money, I'd be able to plunk down the money for the hat. If I tried to buy it now, Hardy would for sure get arrested for disturbing the peace—or for murder.

A little farther down Gold Street, I turned right onto Nugget Road. Marion's narrow, all-brick home sported a wreath of bright springtime flowers on the front door. I pulled into the driveway and decided to see if anyone was home before lugging the basket out of the car. My knock echoed, the sound sad and empty.

I waited a full minute before giving it another try, almost turning away at the twinge of guilt, knowing I wasn't just here to offer comfort but to ask questions. Valorie might have been difficult in the past, typical moody teenager stuff, but I wanted so badly to let her know how my heart hurt for her. Losing one's momma at a young age. . .yeah, I knew something about that.

At long last the sound of soft footsteps let me know someone was on their way. The lock on the door scraped as it retracted, and the door cracked open. Valorie's puffy, teary eyes pinched my heart. The girl clutched the door frame and managed a weak grimace that might have resembled a smile if her bottom lip hadn't trembled.

I spread my arms wide. "No tough-gal stuff for LaTisha. You come here."

Valorie blinked, then blinked again and lunged forward. I caught her in a tight embrace as sobs wracked her slender form.

"That's it, baby, you have a good cry." Valorie's light brown hair tickled my cheek as I cradled her face against my shoulder. All the girl's usual teenage haughtiness had dissolved under the weight of her distress, as I figured it would. Every heart needs another to shelter it when the storms rage.

I closed my eyes, making that tender connection with the Lord and lifting up the broken emotions of my precious bundle. "Lord, you know this hurt." I breathed the prayer, warm and gentle against Valorie's hair. "You know our girl's pain. Comfort her. Wrap your arms around her. Draw her closer to you."

We stood that way for a long time. Finally, Valorie sniffed and pulled back. "Thank you, Mrs. Barnhart."

"Ain't none of that Mrs. stuff. You done wet the front of my dress, and I guess that allows you to call me LaTisha." I held up a finger. "I brought you something to eat. You go on in and I'll fetch it from the car."

In the kitchen, I pulled down a plate, filled it, gave it a spin in the microwave, and made sure Valorie got the fork to her lips a few times. She needed the nourishment. I took a good look around, puzzled by the boxes, some filled, some still empty. "You packing for college?"

Valorie picked at a piece of chicken but didn't meet my eyes. Something was up with that, I was sure. "I can't stay here. I was packing when you rang the bell."

I yanked out a chair and settled myself next to her. "Where you going?"

The old, familiar stubbornness radiated from Valorie's eyes. "I've got a place to stay for a while."

Obviously some great secret, though I suspected Mark Hamm's hug might have something to do with it. Best to let the subject drop. "I want you to know that despite finding your momma, I had nothing to do with it."

Valorie nodded. "Who would—?" She picked up her glass of water and sipped.

"I don't know, baby, but I'm doing my best to figure things out."

Valorie slanted me a look. "Chief Conrad's in

charge. He's thinking it might have been more than a bad fall."

"You're right about that," I agreed.

"Then what are you doing?"

"I'm trying to piece things together. My college courses give me a natural interest, so I figured I'd get to work doing what I could, in an unofficial capacity, if you know what I mean."

Valorie stabbed a dumpling and examined it, but she couldn't hide the tremble of her lips. "My mom wasn't a real nice person most of the time."

"Your momma had her problems. We all do." The time had come to ask the question raised by the report of her mother's displeasure over her cheating. "Do *you* think she tripped and fell?"

Valorie abandoned her efforts to eat and stared down at her hands clasped in her lap. "I don't know what to think." She swiped at her face and sniffed.

This girl had something on her mind.

A young girl loses her mother—what, besides grief, would she struggle with? Her mother pushed her, yes. Marion always wanted Valorie to be the best and do the best. . . . Did that set a bomb ticking in Valorie's brain? Would her resentment over her mother's hovering anger her enough to push her mother into that radiator? What if it was an accident? One of those moments of pure rage that one lived to regret forever?

With two girls of my own, it's not hard for me to understand that a mother's hopes and dreams for her daughters are different than those for her sons. I recalled the one time I had pushed Shayna to get her degree in something other than business management. For two years Shayna held her ground, resisting my suggestion. "Momma, it's what I want. Why can't you let me be me? I'm the one who has to live with my decision."

Such a simple statement of fact. No anger. Just a deep sorrow that radiated from my girl as she petitioned me with what I knew to be true.

Hardy's words from the previous night flashed in my mind. We had indeed raised our babies to be independent, with the attitude that they could do anything they put their minds to, and that God had blessed each of them with a good mind, so they most certainly had better use it.

How much more pressure would there be on an only child? Especially from Marion. I liked to think that I wasn't quite as pushy. Truth was, my girls would probably say I was.

I touched Valorie's shoulder. "Your momma wanted you to be the best you could be. You might not have always liked it, and that's okay." Beneath my hand, her narrow shoulders twitched and heaved.

"I tried to please her."

"You admitted that you cheated in Ms. Letzburg's class."

Valorie nodded, head bowed, hands tightly clenched in her lap. "Straight As was all she cared about. I always struggled in Ms. Letzburg's class. So. . .I began cheating on the tests."

"Did you tell your momma the truth first, or did

she find out from Ms. Letzburg?"

"I tried." She snatched up her napkin and dabbed at her eyes. "She didn't believe me! Always thought I was so smart. Maybe she didn't want to believe me. I think she wanted me to do so well because she never learned to read well and always had to ask me for help with the books. It embarrassed her."

I glanced around the small but elegant kitchen. Its rich cherry cabinets and granite countertops gleamed with good care. The house gave off a showroom-quality feel.

Superficial.

Beneath all the bravado and attitude, Marion's secret must have haunted her. It explained the reason she always gave me the store's paperwork to do and asked me to read off the inventory list.

Valorie stood up and wiped her eyes again. "I've got to get back to packing. My. . ." She hesitated. "My friend will be here any minute."

"You take those dumplings with you and share them. No sense in leaving them here to spoil."

Valorie's head dipped once, and a slow, shy smile curved her lips. "Thank you. For everything."

"Not necessary." I huffed to my feet. "I'm here for you, baby. Willing and wanting to help." Once again I gathered the slender form to myself and whispered in her ear. "God loves you."

On the front porch, the sun glinted off the windshield of a car as it slowed at the driveway but kept going. Valorie licked her lips, her eyes darting to me.

Feigning disinterest in the car, or Valorie's reaction, I squeezed the girl's hand. As soon as I backed out of the driveway, I aimed Old Lou down Nugget Road and onto Gold Street where the strip of buildings included the grocery and Regina Rogane's salon.

From my parallel parking spot in front of the grocery, I could see down Nugget Road to the front of Marion's home. Just as I grabbed a cart and entered the grocery, the same car that had slowed by the driveway minutes earlier pulled in.

Mark Hamm got out.

9

The aisles of the Bright Sky Grocery remained relatively free of patrons. Passing the display of oranges and apples, I rounded the end of the fruit display toward Shiny Portley's little stainless steel cart where he stood and sliced fresh pineapple into juicy, sweet chunks. Made my mouth water just watching him.

As the owner of the store, he made it a habit of being out where the customers could see him and ask questions about his products. I tried to hide my amusement at the bright reflection off Shiny's bald head as he worked the knife. Shiny's nickname served him well. Come to think of it, so did his last name. He grinned at me as I parked my cart next to his workstation.

"You can't resist this fruity sunshine, LaTisha Barnhart."

"Mmm, and you knows how much Hardy loves his pineapple. I'll take that one. Can't get any fresher than that."

Shiny slid the golden chunks into a plastic container and slapped a price sticker onto the side. Deep creases formed along his eyes as the corners of his mouth curved into a smile. His laugh shook his belly. "My pleasure, LaTisha. Tell Hardy to save a piece of the pineapple upside-down cake for us poor single grocers." He rubbed a hand over his belly and smacked his lips.

"No sense in hinting around. You give me a free

container of that pineapple, and I'll deliver your cake tomorrow."

He held out the one in his hand. "Deal!"

As I put it in my basket, Shiny leaned closer and lowered his voice. "Who do you think did Marion in?"

I leaned toward him and grated out my reply. "I did. Don't tell."

He tilted his head to look into my eyes. "I imagine there's someone with a lot more reason than you, LaTisha. Even with her firing you and everything."

"You talkin' foolish. I quit that job 'cause Marion tried to boss me once too much."

Shiny bobbed his head. "Yeah, I can understand that. One time she came into the store with Valorie and demanded to know why the sell-by date on my milk wasn't as fresh as the Grab-N-Go."

"You should've told her to buy her own cow."

"I told her if Grab-N-Go was so much fresher, go buy her milk there and leave me alone."

I wagged my finger at him. "You keep talking like that, and everyone'll think you have a motive."

He leaned in again. "Between you and me, I think old Payton had enough of her mouth. That whole thing about Marion's building being a historical site might be true, but not every old building can be saved. Marion sure didn't have a problem selling when the contractor waved the money under her nose."

"Let me lay this one on you. You have any idea why Mark Hamm recused his vote?"

Shiny shrugged and selected another pineapple. "He's a strange bird." His blade winked and flashed, then descended with a solid thunk. "Don't know about him. Must have something to do with the whole mess. Valorie sure seems to like him."

As Shiny lifted the knife for another whack, I had the strange urge to holler, "Hei-yah!" As good as his aim was, maybe I should hire him to work on my bunions. He'd take his pay in pineapple upside-down cakes.

He pointed with his knife in the direction of the west wall, beyond which lay Wig Out, Regina Rogane's salon. "You know who has their ear to the ground is Regina. She knows most everything that goes on in this town, even the hush-hush, because she's around gabbing women all day. And with all the spats she and Marion had over the politics of Maple Gap, I wouldn't doubt for a minute that somewhere down deep, she has a motive for giving Marion the push."

"Our good police chief would caution you not to jump to that conclusion."

He waved his knife in the air. "I know, I know. She could have just fallen onto that radiator. But you know as well as I do, and everyone else in town, that she was pushed. I'd bet my new toupee on it."

I arched my brows. Shiny's last attempt with a toupee had left the entire town in stitches for three weeks before he finally decided to give it up for Lent.

"Why don't you grow your eyebrows extra long and comb them upward? That might work."

He grimaced as he scooted more pineapple chunks into a container. "Very funny. Don't be forgetting my cake, either."

10

You get yourself down here right now, Hardy Barnhart. I'm not waitin' on you another minute. No way am I gonna be late again for another Wednesday prayer service. You hear me? You're as slow as a wart dissolvin'."

"And you're bossier than a whole army of drill instructors."

"You get your sorry self down here and let me look at you before we leave. Genghis Khan knows you've probably got on those plaid pants I keep tryin' to hide." I glared at the ceiling, waiting for the telltale creak of the floorboards or the scuff of socked feet that heralded his appearance.

Nothing.

He'd probably worn himself out hiking his britches up and decided to lay down across the bed. I'd fix him. Grabbing the broom I kept leaned against the hall table for just such occasions, I thumped the stick straight up into the ceiling three times.

A thud on the floor right where the bed was located proved me right. Hardy's voice howled down the steps. "I'm coming. Don't you put a hole in that ceiling, neither. I've done patched enough of your broom handle holes to last me a lifetime."

"You're not gonna have any life left if you're not down here lickety quick."

Hardy appeared at the top of the steps, polyester pants riding high.

"Woo-wee! For sure you'd better yank them things down, or you'll be singing high tenor at church."

He sent me one of his long-suffering grins. "I like them this way."

I shook my head, pursed my lips, and heaved a dramatic sigh. Love him or leave him. And I loved him too much, high tenor or not. "No time now for me to be stewing about you—we gotta get."

Hardy turned toward the hall mirror and adjusted his tie. "I look pretty good for an old man."

"To someone with bad vision."

"Your vision's pretty good."

"Until I get a good look at that plaid—then I go cross-eyed."

He shot a glance at my pillbox hat. "You stir up any trouble today?"

"What you meanin'? The only trouble I stir is when I smack your lazy bones off that sofa."

His lips formed a firm line. "That's your trouble hat. You only wear that thing when you've done something you ain't proud of." Hardy spit in his hands, focused his brandy eyes in the mirror above the hall table, and tried to smooth the grizzled edges of his hair. "How's Valorie doin'?"

I slicked a hand down the back of Hardy's head, where a clump of hair rose from the rest like a ghost in a graveyard. "She cried like a baby in my arms."

He raised his bushy brows.

"She's a sweet thing down inside. Her momma pushed her so hard to succeed, it made her angry. Valorie's beside herself with grief. Mark Hamm pulled in after I left."

Hardy scooped up his keys and opened the door for me. "Mark?"

"She was packing her clothes. Told me she had a place to go, and then Mark shows up."

"See? Told you that hat spelled trouble. You were spying on them."

" 'Course not." Wiggling my toes, I felt the crease of my hose wearing against my small toe and kicked off my shoe to straighten it out. "I can't help it that I saw him pull into her driveway."

"Mmm-hmm."

He opened the door for me and locked it, pocketing his key with a little difficulty.

"You didn't wear them things so tight and high, you'd have room to wiggle your fingers in your pocket."

"You leave my pants alone."

He opened the car door for me, so I waited to continue the conversation until he rounded the front of Old Lou and got in.

"What I said is true enough. As I was leaving Valorie's house, a car slowed down right in front of us, then kept going. You know the grocery store looks right down that road. From there I could see when Mark's car pulled in."

"Maybe he wanted to check on her."

"No, there's more to it than that. You mark my words. And I aim to find out what's going on there."

We rode the rest of the way in silence. Almost silence, except for the chug and grate of Old Lou's engine mirroring the rhythm of my thoughts. Despite my best efforts, I wasn't learning much. Plenty of people had motives for wanting Marion dead, or at least intimidated by a hard shove that unfortunately ended in death. And if that was the case, someone must be really scared. I wonder how Miss Marple would handle a crime like this?

Observation.

Keeping my mouth shut and my eyes open might glean some information, and since almost everyone I could think of went to Maple Gap's church on Wednesdays, I should be able to observe everyone in action.

As Hardy pulled up in front of the redbrick church to let me out, my eyes landed smack dab on the back of Officer Mac Simpson and his conversational companion, Dana Letzburg. *Hmm.* Body language spoke volumes, and Dana's wrote a book. She sidled sideways away from Mac. He continued to talk. Looked to me like the boy needed to cool his heels.

While Hardy parked, I scooted toward the front door. A child went racing by, followed by another towheaded boy. I snatched at the quickly departing shirttail and managed to grab hold of Tanner Murphy, my Sunday school student. Recipient of many classes on manners and about to become a living example of what happens when boys don't pay attention in my class.

He hollered as I reeled him in and turned his big brown eyes on me. I smiled and motioned to his brother, who had stopped to find out what Tanner was squawking about.

"I'll thank you, boys, for not running. You run over one of us old people, and you're liable to get squashed." I shook my head. "Not a pretty way to die, Tanner. Right, Mickey?"

They shared a look and nodded at me.

"There you are." Their mother, Belinda Murphy, hair blown every which way, hurried up the sidewalk. Belinda Murphy's naturally high color lent her the look of an athlete. I knew the woman to be a hard worker. Chasing after these boys probably qualified her for the Olympic five-hundred-yard sprint. Her eyes narrowed at her sons. "Can't you two stay out of trouble for a minute?"

Tanner and Mickey sent one more glance my way. I gave them my best you'd-better-polish-your-halos-and-be-quick-about-it look. In unison, they nodded, and by some prerehearsed miracle, the boys each took one of their mother's hands. Maybe I wouldn't give them the write-it-a-hundred-times punishment I'd had in mind.

Belinda released Tanner's hand long enough to brush back a strand of her tousled hair. "I don't know how you do it, Mrs. Barnhart."

"They're good boys, Belinda. They listen." *Most of the time.* "You've done a fine job with them, and don't you forget it."

"Thank you." She grimaced. "With Jack gone all

the time, it's tough sometimes."

I patted the younger woman's shoulder. "I remember those days when Hardy had to leave for weeks at a time. It grows you as a person. Now. . ." I raised my voice a bit to make sure the boys heard my next words. "I've got a huge caramel-pecan cake that needs eaten. You think you and your boys would like to take it off my hands?"

Tanner stared up at his mother with longing eyes. Mickey, the bolder of the two, tugged on her arm. "Please, Mom? Can we?"

"That's very nice of you, LaTisha. You must be missing Lela. Caramel-pecan's her favorite, isn't it?"

The thrust of that question swept the breath from my lungs. Missing Lela more than a flea missed a good dog. "You come on by tonight after service, and we'll hand it off to you and your boys."

Mickey did a little dance while Tanner smiled his appreciation. Belinda tried to settle them with a look. "What do you say, boys?"

"Is it a whole cake?" Tanner piped up.

I chuckled at Belinda's horrified look.

"It's a whole cake," I assured the young man.

As the buzzer signaling five minutes until service sounded, Belinda and I herded the boys through the doors and toward the sanctuary.

A light touch on my arm let me know Hardy had made his appearance, seconds before his voice whispered toward my ear.

"You missed the whole thing between that young

officer and Dana. I think he was trying to ask her out and she was playing hard to get. When Payton came in, she went right to him."

I didn't turn my head, for fear my stare might alert Payton and Dana to my interest. I patted Hardy's hand on my elbow and dragged him forward through a maze of people and a hailstorm of greetings before we arrived at our usual spot.

Immediately, Sara Anne Buchanan, age ten, was at my side and primed for a hug. I pulled the slender body against my shoulder. For two years, the little lady had struggled with leukemia. Before Lela had gone to college, they had declared Sara in remission—all praise to the Lord—but the girl still felt too thin. Her complexion still too pale for my liking.

Lela and I had taken turns going with Sara's mother and father to the chemotherapy treatments. Between the two of us, we made sure the Buchanans ate well.

I stroked the hair back from her forehead. "Sweet girl. How's my baby?"

"I miss Lela," Sara whispered.

Two reminders of my empty nest in one evening. My heart ached from the onslaught. I paused to fight back the demons of the depression that tugged on me. "I miss her, too." Best to get my mind on Sara and off myself.

"I got a secret. You can't tell." I stared into her blue, blue eyes and waited for the sparkle of excitement to shine before I continued. "I made some beef stew last night. Would you like to share some?"

"Yum! Can I? I'd better ask my mom. She'll probably say yes 'cause I got a good grade on my test at school today. Know what else? I got picked first at recess!"

Pastor Haudaire took his place behind the podium.

"Wonderful, baby. You ask your momma." I winked and gave her another hug. "Tell me what she says after service. Okay?"

Sara leaned in for another hug and a quick "I love you" before she slipped out into the aisle and down two pews to her mother's side.

"You keep this up," Hardy whispered from my other side, "and we're going to have to build a drive-through window onto the kitchen."

"Give you some good hard work to do to keep you from harassing me. Now you hush up and let me listen to this music." I crossed my arms and leaned back in the pew as the first chords of organ music filled the air.

Hardy slid his arm along the back of the pew and around my shoulders. The gentle press of his body against me swelled my sense of satisfaction. I put my hand over his knee and gave a gentle pat.

The song leader appeared and with the tilt of his hand invited the congregation to rise and join in a chorus. I reared my head back and let loose. Hardy often warned me about outhonking everyone within a three-pew range, but he conceded that my voice sounded like velvet against the skin. Besides, this is how I worshipped. My surroundings and my cares faded under the flow of the song.

Chief Conrad stopped me after the last amen. He didn't look happy. I tried to land my eyes on Officer Simpson to see if the young man might be lurking, waiting to see the ax fall on my neck for my shenanigans earlier in the day.

No sign of Mac anywhere.

I slid another glance at the chief. Was he going to arrest me? I pushed the thought away.

Dana stood alone in the center aisle, no sign of Payton anywhere. I got a glimpse of Mark Hamm and a vulnerable-looking Valorie as they scooted through the already-dispersing crowd and out the doors.

Sara came barreling up the aisle toward me, Tanner and Mickey on her heels. Sara reached me first, pausing long enough to give Chief Conrad a shy wave.

"My mom said I could have the stew." She rubbed her nonexistent tummy, eyes twinkling.

"You let me talk to the chief, and we'll leave for my house right away." I raised my eyes to Conrad. "Unless I can lure the officer to my house with the promise of a slice of cherry pie."

Mickey piped up, his eyes solemn as he addressed the police chief. "Me and Tanner get some cake. A whole cake. Just us, 'cause Mom's on a diet."

Chief Conrad tousled Tanner's hair. "A whole cake? Not even a slice for me?"

Tanner gave Mickey an uncertain look.

"No, sir," Mickey said, totally unruffled. "She

promised it to us, didn't you, Mrs. Barnhart?"

"Sure did," I said, still a little worried about the chief's intentions in singling me out.

Chief's expression lost some of its somberness. "I think I'll take you up on the offer, LaTisha. What I need to ask you would probably be better discussed in private anyhow."

I agonized over what those questions might be the entire drive home. Not even Hardy's carrying on with the boys—who begged to ride in Old Lou—distracted me enough to grant me ease.

As soon as we landed in the driveway, the two boys raced to the side door. Hardy laughed. "Ain't in a hurry, are you, fellas?"

I put the cake in a carrier and handed it to Belinda when she arrived. Right off, Mickey and Tanner began to argue over who would hold it. I bid the boys good-bye and waited for my next customer, feeling very much like a drive-through worker.

Chief Conrad arrived next. Sara and her parents parked right behind his car. This time Hardy handed the food over as I prepared a generous slice of the cherry pie for the chief.

"She's such a frail thing," Hardy began as he came inside after seeing Sara off. "Her mother told me to thank you. Seems Sara doesn't eat anything as well as she eats your cooking."

"I'll have to fry up a passel of chicken for her. She sure loves my chicken."

Hardy's smile took the edge off my fear. "Make

enough for me, too."

I spooned a generous helping of ice cream onto the pie and nodded to the coffee machine. "Run me a cup for the chief."

"Sure thing."

Placing a spoon on the plate, I headed to the living room, where Chief Conrad scanned the day-old paper. He appeared more relaxed, less dutiful than at the church.

"No one makes pie like you do," he said as he accepted the dish. "It sure wouldn't hurt for you to open up a restaurant. You'd probably put Mark out of business."

"Don't think he'd appreciate that too much."

"No, but the folks around here would sure love it."

As Chief Conrad took a generous bite of pie, I settled my bulk into my favorite recliner. "The paper's full of Marion." He pointed with his spoon at the folded paper. "Makes my head spin to keep up with what everyone is saying."

"You're not convinced she was pushed?"

Conrad's spoon stilled in midair. He seemed to consider my question a minute, then followed through with another bite of pie. He chewed slowly, little concentration-creases forming between his brows. "Well, I suppose not. We're still waiting on the test results, you know. But off the record, it sure looks like it was no accident." He set his dish on the coffee table. "The depth of her wound is what has me thinking it wasn't a simple fall. The radiator she bashed her head against could have knocked her out, sure, but not killed her."

"Do you have any theories?"

Conrad leaned forward and cut another bite with the edge of his fork. "I do, but none I can share right now. Which leads me to the questions I needed to ask you."

I sucked in air and let it out slow and easy. "I'm ready."

"It's nothing like you think, LaTisha. You have a concrete alibi. The librarian confirmed that you were there. I checked it out yesterday."

I can tell you that news tickled my ears real good. My breath came easier. "So what you here for?"

"What I need is help. You know the budget has everything tight and"—he grimaced—"Officer Simpson isn't quite used to the folks around here yet, so they won't give him the time of day. But you. . ."

He held such a hopeful expression. My mind clattered along with the possibilities of what he was suggesting.

"With all those courses you're taking and you being a native and all, no one will shrink from you asking them questions. But I can't pay you, LaTisha. It's not in the budget, and I—" He winced. "I'd need you to keep low-key. If the state police or the rest of our officers found out I was doing this, well, I might have some real problems."

I needed no further prodding. "I'll do what I can. I hear there's a reward."

He brightened. "That's true. A private citizen posted a thousand-dollar reward. If you help nail the criminal, it's yours."

"You know who it was who posted it?"

He ran his finger around the edge of his plate. "Can't tell you because I don't know."

Beans! Curiosity was gonna kill me for sure. "What do you want me to begin with?"

Chief Conrad scooped up the last bite of his pie and swished it around in the puddle of melted ice cream before popping it into his mouth. Hardy entered, walking carefully as he carried a full cup of coffee. He set it down in front of the officer.

"You like it black?"

"Black is fine. Thank you, Hardy."

Hardy plopped onto the opposite end of the sofa from the chief. "So you hauling my wife off to jail?"

I gave him a withering glance.

"No, Hardy." Chief Conrad laughed. "You'll have to put up with her for a while longer, I'm afraid. Her alibi—and yours as well, I might add—check out. I was just asking your wife if she would agree to help me out, but this is a private agreement between her and me. Word of it can't leave this room."

Hardy grinned. "It's about time. She's one mighty smart woman."

"Yes, I know." Conrad relaxed back into the cushions and crossed his ankles. "The first person I need your input on is Regina Rogane. I received an anonymous tip that her cessation from the mayoral campaign a few years back was not totally voluntary. You remember the scandal over the missing money?"

"Regina resigned shortly afterward, citing problems

with people on the committee. Lots of people wondered if it meant she'd been guilty of taking the campaign funds," I said.

"Can you talk to her, LaTisha? Find out what happened and if Marion's place on the committee ties in with Regina quitting so suddenly. I want as many details of that scandal as possible."

Wig Out, Regina's hair salon, smelled like a perm Thursday morning. The stench was nearly intolerable. Terrible what women—black or white—did to their hair. Between perms, relaxers, heat pressing, and blow dryers, it was a wonder more of us weren't plucked bald.

I always wanted to be one of those black women brave enough to let her hair go natural. But I doggedly maintained my regimen of relaxing it once every two months. Any more frequently than that and my hair broke off quicker than it grew. Shayna had been the one to encourage me to extend my treatment to once every ten weeks. "Your hair will love you for it."

Last summer, Lela and I surrendered our home relaxing regimen in favor of letting Regina do the honors. Regina studied up on the processes for African-American hair and assured both Lela and me we would be safe in her hands. Both of us had been impressed with Regina's extensive knowledge and had loved the products she used. So I kept coming back.

As I closed the door on the bright morning sun and faced the room, I switched mental gears and vowed to listen closely to the conversations that flowed between Regina and her patrons. I breathed in the rancid odor saturating the air of Regina's shop and raised my hand in greeting.

"Hey there, lady!" Regina said between snips of her scissors.

Regina Rogane could put a hurtin' on most women if she had a mind to. Tall, the woman radiated good health and plenty of exercise. Chatty and upbeat, I could see where her sunshine personality would be a slow burn on the delicate skin of someone like Marion.

"I'll be with you in a few minutes, LaTisha. Just let me finish up," Regina said as she enthusiastically began to tease the hair of the only other patron in the shop. One of Maple Gap's finest—at least in her own mind. Mrs. Eugene Taser. The mayor's wife of Maple Gap, and don't you forget it.

"Hello, LaTisha," Mrs. Taser began. "It's terrible to hear of Marion's death. I suppose you know more than anyone about the details."

"I know what I saw, Betsy." I waddled my way over to the chairs and eyeballed one with arms. It looked like a torture device for anyone over a size twelve. Double that for me, honey, and you can see my concern.

The mayor's wife frowned at my casual use of her first name. I settled into another chair, one without arms, and smiled widely at Betsy's chagrin. She much preferred to be addressed as "Mrs. Taser," which was the exact reason I called her Betsy.

I decided to restart the conversation with pleasantries. "How's Eugene?"

"The *mayor* is doing fine."

Behind Betsy's head, Regina rolled her eyes toward the ceiling.

"How's your mother doing, Regina?"

Regina's eyes shifted over to me for a split second before she set aside the comb and began wrapping Mrs. Taser's teased puffs into loose rolls. "She's getting worse."

I remembered Regina's mother with great fondness. Though a good twenty-five years my senior, Eloise Rogane had been an involved resident of Maple Gap and a wonderful neighbor. Alzheimer's had too quickly taken its terrible toll.

"It must be very hard. I know how you struggled with the decision to put her in assisted living."

"She requires full-time care now," Regina said, her expression stoic. I recognized her attempt to maintain her composure. Her hands flew from one tuft of hair to another as she unrolled, combed, and pinned. Unrolled, combed, and pinned.

Mrs. Taser, obviously more attuned to our conversation than to the magazine in her lap, piped up. "She probably won't last much longer, dear; then you'll be free."

Regina broke pace, eyes flashing at the back of the woman's head, then up at me in silent misery. In the next instant, Regina swooped up the can of hairspray and doused Mrs. Taser's hair from all angles—maybe a little too much in the front. Mrs. Taser gasped and choked.

"You trying to asphyxiate me?"

Regina ripped off the protective cape and declared with more energy than necessary, "You're all done!"

Betsy Taser rose, still coughing, and rounded on

Regina. "You didn't even let me look at myself first to see if I approved. I must always look my best."

"There's no hope, honey," I ground out. "You'd better take what Regina gives you and be happy."

The woman stiffened and glared. "Well!"

Regina put her hand across her mouth.

Betsy's eyes narrowed at the hairdresser. "Put it on my tab, as usual."

Regina's face immediately lost its animation, sinking into what I thought to be a look of resignation. "Have a nice day."

I smiled up at Betsy as she hovered by the door, green eyes flashing down at me. "Laughter is good for the spirit, sister. Don't take everything so seriously. Lighten up and be free!"

Betsy sputtered then pulled her purse strap onto her shoulder and slammed out of the salon, or she would have if not for one of those elbow-thingie hinges that made the door close softly.

Regina and I exchanged bemused looks and burst into laughter.

She squirted some liquid soap and began working her hands together. "She is so egotistical."

"Goes with being a politician. Or the wife of one. Not that I'd know personally."

Regina tugged a towel down from the rack above the sink and dried her hands. "Believe me, even during the campaign she was like that. Her dad was a politician, too. Maybe that explains it."

Something about the conversation between Regina

and Betsy stirred around in my head. "Do you send her a bill or something?"

Regina wound the towel around her right hand. "Something like that. So what will it be for you today?"

I squinted at the girl. Funny she should ask now; she always asked when appointments were made, so she could be prepared. Maybe she'd forgotten. I touched my hair. "Full treatment this time. Though I'm tempted to do dreads and forget the whole thing."

Regina broke into a wide grin. "You'd be the talk of the town, but somehow it would be fitting for you to have dreads. Wonder what Hardy would say?"

I howled at that. "He'd say, 'Tisha, ain't no sense in you looking like you got carpet burn in your hair.' You know what I've always wanted to try? Those microbreads. Shayna got them done at Christmastime and looked real good. A little head heavy—all them beads swingin' and dancin' about—but good."

"You'd probably get a headache." Regina snapped the pink plastic cape around my neck after I settled my bulk into the chair. "I just ordered a copy of *African-American Hairstyles*. Why don't you give it a look-see?"

I followed the hairdresser's path with my eyes toward the back room. Regina returned in a wink with a glossy, pristine magazine in hand and dropped it into my lap. A close-up of a black woman sporting a natural look on the front tempted me.

"I looked through it briefly," Regina said. "Lots of Bantu knots and microbreads. They must be all the rage. See what you can find and we'll schedule another appointment to get you your new look."

"You sure it won't be more than you can handle?"

"Nope. I can figure out most anything. And when I go to visit my mother, they have a hair salon especially for African-American women right near Mom's home. I can pop in and ask someone to give me some pointers if I need to."

I spread the magazine on my lap and thought about the offer. I loved my hats and never gave too much thought to my hair. Flattening it with a hot iron after a wash always seemed sufficient care. Maybe I should try something new. With no kids to fuss after, I could afford to have a more high-maintenance type of hairdo.

"My mom always said a woman should have a hairstyle that makes her feel like wow," Regina said.

Yes. I'd heard Eloise make that comment before. "My hats usually make me feel that way."

"Maybe because you've been trying to hide your hair."

"Never thought of it that way," I conceded.

Regina busied herself dabbing olive oil on my hair.

"I'm sorry to hear about your momma being worse, Regina."

She flicked a smile and tilted the chair backward to begin washing. The warm water flowed over my head, relaxing me. "Maybe I'll shake Hardy's bones long enough to get him to haul me over to see her." I closed my eyes and imagined myself standing under the soft spray of a warm waterfall, surrounded by woods and cute forest animals.

"I don't know, LaTisha. Mom's pretty bad."

I heard the catch in the girl's voice and my illusion dissolved. Poor girl. "Shayna's coming to town. I'll have her pop in."

Regina cleared her throat. "I'd love to see her. She dating anyone?"

"Some guy she met her senior year of college. Apparently he works downstairs in her building, and they ran into each other so frequently, they decided they might as well get to know each other better. It's been three months."

"She bringing him home?"

Regina massaged in another dose of shampoo.

I always forgot how much I enjoyed having someone else do my hair until Regina's fingers started circular motions on my scalp. "She said she was. We'll see." I wasn't sure, but it sounded a little like my words were slurring together.

"Any other children coming home this spring?"

"For Easter supper. Shakespeare, Bryton and Fredlynn, Mason, Shayna, and Caleb are the only ones able to come this time."

"I imagine Lela is bogged down with her new classes. I sure miss that girl. How's Shakespeare's teaching?"

"Fine. Know what I worry about most? Him not dating anyone. Ever since he got out of college and broke off his engagement, he doesn't seem interested. But his teaching is going fine. Hardy's mighty proud of him. They'll probably go over to Payton's and bang around on those pianos the entire time he's home."

"He sure has talent. Think he'll go professional?"

"Naw. His heart is more in teaching than playing on that level. I'd be happy with him settling down and giving me some grandbabies."

"Cora doing okay?"

"That's why they're not coming. Tyrone's afraid for her to travel so close to her due date. Says Cora's exhausted all the time. I told that boy he'd better remember who got her where she is and take good care of her."

"If all your kids get married and have as many babies as you did, you'll have to hire someone to help you with grandparenting duties."

"Nope. I'll love them all myself. When I get tired, I'll have their grandpappy play them to sleep."

Regina dabbed my hair dry and pushed my chair upright with a grunt. I blinked my eyes open. Reopening the magazine, I leafed through it as Regina spun my chair to face the mirror.

"Woo-wee, would you look at that." I lifted the magazine so Regina could see the picture of a stylish woman with an updo. "That's pretty."

Regina leaned closer to get a good look at the picture. "I can do that, LaTisha."

I tried to picture the style on top of my head. "No. Probably too much work. Looks like something Marion would go for."

"May she rest in peace."

"She surely didn't hand it out to anyone while she was living. Heard about funeral arrangements yet?"

"Saturday at noon," Regina said. "I told Valorie she should get you to sing."

"Me?"

"Sure. No one sings 'Amazing Grace' like you."

I lifted a hand to wipe a drop of water tickling on my forehead. "No one feels it like I do." It was time to begin gathering some information from Regina. "What is the gossip on Marion's death?"

"Most think Mark Hamm is a bit suspicious. I've thought it ever since he came to town. Weird with a capital *W*." She shook her head. Her hands patted the towel over my hair to absorb water. "One day, I saw him hanging around outside the shop and wondered what he was up to. I was cutting Valorie's hair at the time. He didn't say anything to Valorie that I know of, but came in after she left looking real embarrassed. Of course, every eye in the shop popped when he came in. I'd just cleaned out the brushes I'd used on her and swept up the clippings. Was about to dump the dustpan when he got real close and asked me if he could have some. Can you believe that?"

She indicated the back room with a roll of her head. "He followed me back there, and just as I lifted the lid to dump the stuff, he waved a fifty under my nose. I was shocked. Before I knew it, he added another fifty. Well, with the cost of Momma's care, I can tell you that was way too much temptation for this gal. I let him pick some out of the dustpan. He stuffed it into an envelope. Went straight for the door after that."

"Hmm," was all I inserted. This sister was on a roll,

and what she said really spun some questions around in my head.

Regina moved back and forth a few times, squirting and dabbing conditioner on my hair before snagging a wide-toothed comb. She carefully sectioned my hair and began the comb-out. "You want to do braid-outs?"

"Sounds good." When her eyebrows came together in concentration, I decided to prompt her or she might never finish her story. "What happened next?"

"Well, I didn't tell the girls what I'd done, but we sure talked over the strange request after he left. Most of the women thought he was some kind of stalker, and now, with the way he parades around with Valorie. . ." She caught my eye in the mirror. "Kind of makes you wonder, doesn't it?"

"I can assure you Marion didn't approve. Some think it's been going on for a while." I tried to picture Mark Hamm in a fit of rage, pushing Marion. Or Valorie doing the pushing. . . Maybe Valorie's grief was tinged with guilt? In light of this new information, her declaration that she had a place to stay seemed frightfully bold. But young girls lost their heads over older men every day. If Marion had caused a flap and forbidden Valorie from seeing Mark. . .

Regina's hands stilled mid-comb. "Love is a powerful motive."

Chills ran up my back. "I was thinking along those same lines."

Were Valorie and Mark in cahoots? I'd have to shelve that information for a while and think on it later. While interesting to know, I reminded myself that I still had questions about Regina that needed answering. Was the story she shared about Mark a way to detour everyone's suspicions from her?

Time to spill a little of the information I'd become privy to and test the waters a bit. "I heard there was an envelope of money on the counter at Marion's. Heard anyone mention that? Chief collected it and is waiting on the results of a fingerprint test."

The easy rhythm of Regina's comb-out faltered. Her eyes flashed something akin to panic before she dipped her head and resumed combing. "Now that you mention it, the police did question me on the presence of an envelope. Wonder what it was."

I returned to looking through the magazine, trying to decide exactly what had shaken up Regina and why she was trying so hard to act nonchalant. Bigger question—why hadn't Chief mentioned that he'd questioned her about the envelope? Maybe he'd forgotten.

A gust of air signaled the arrival of another customer. I wiggled my fingers as Sasha Blightman blew in with the warm breeze that swirled through the shop. "Howdy, ladies. Saw you salivating as you drove by, LaTisha. Like that sweet little hat in the window?"

"That hat tempts me every time I see it. Surprised you didn't sell it during your sidewalk sale."

Sasha, ever the fashion plate, tugged on the pastel scarf serving as a belt and let out a groan. "That was a fiasco."

Regina smiled at Sasha in the mirror. "I did my best to help keep you out of Chapter 11."

Sasha trilled a laugh. "Sales weren't the problem. Hauling everything in and out is the tedious part. Since sales were so good, we extended it through Monday. You'll have to hurry over and try on that hat, LaTisha. I'll give you a good discount."

She faced Regina as she slipped her perfect size eight form into one of the three chairs. "Olivia was disappointed you couldn't fit her in today. We thought maybe something had happened to your mother when you canceled our appointments on Tuesday. It turned out to be a blessing, though, because a delivery arrived at ten and it took us until lunchtime to get everything put out."

Ten o'clock until noon. The time frame of Marion's death. I forced myself not to react to the news and studied Regina. Her expression remained neutral, though I thought I saw a slight tightening of her lips.

She snapped a plastic cap around my head. "Sorry, Sasha. I had a long lunch date."

12

I mulled over Sasha's interesting announcement in my kitchen as I mixed, then baked, Shiny's pineapple upside-down cake. After dropping it off, still warm from the oven, I backtracked to Mark Hamm's restaurant. Standing there, smelling the grease from Mark's restaurant, I wondered about the future health of the high-cholesterol patients inside. *Lord, forgive me for desecrating my body with greasy fast food.* The only products on Mark's menu I'd ever condescend to eat were his onion rings and salad—and lettuce settled worse in my stomach than tea.

I pulled open the door, imagining myself cutting through a cloud scented with grease and onions. A sign propped against the greeting station blared, in neon lettering, COOK WANTED.

Tammy greeted me. A tall, slender girl who graduated with Lela, Tammy remained in Maple Gap working to save enough to attend community college in the fall.

"How you doing, Mrs. Barnhart?"

"Fine, baby, how're you?"

"Pinching pennies and saving dimes." Tammy poised to slide a menu from the holder on the wall and stopped. "You have the usual?"

"Just some rings. I'd really like to talk to Mark."

Tammy shrugged. "Okay. I'll put in the order. You

have a seat wherever you like."

I had a tough choice. Between heavily varnished Americana furniture and green vinyl booths—I went against my better judgment and took the booth. Never did make the things wide enough for my liking, but it would be more private should other townsfolk come in for an early dinner.

As soon as my rear made contact, the vinyl let out an embarrassing squeal of air. Didn't even have Hardy with me to lay blame on. With a push, I forced the table away to allow myself more room to maneuver into the narrow space.

Mark appeared at my side. His tall, lean frame a direct contrast to the fat content of the food he prepared daily. Handsome enough, though, even for a guy at least twenty years Valorie's senior. This time, as I looked him over, something about the firm set of his lips jogged my memory, as if I'd seen that same look elsewhere, on someone else. Strange. I'd never before had that impression. Why now?

His smile revealed a nice flash of white teeth. Reminded me that I needed to make an appointment for Hardy. Dentures, ya know.

"What can I do for you, LaTisha?"

"Have a seat, first of all. Don't need a crick in my neck from straining to see ya."

His expression became guarded, and I knew he must be wondering if I'd seen him yesterday. That's when a lightbulb lit in my brain, giving me an idea how I could get more information from this closemouthed man. I gave myself a mental pat on the back and launched into my speech. "You see, I—uh—am looking for a job, and you're looking for a cook. I can do all that and you know it. I've fed this town for years right out of my own kitchen."

Mark sat down and stretched his feet into the aisle. "Well, now. That's some kind of résumé."

"Ain't a body here who, when they took sick, hasn't had them a pot of LaTisha's chicken soup delivered right to their doorstep."

Tammy entered the dining area and began filling salt and pepper shakers and replacing the paper napkins of breakfast and lunch with cloth ones for the dinner rush.

Mark rubbed his chin. "Rumor is Marion fired you."

That again. "I quit, and my alibi is airtight, if that's where your mind is headed." *Which is more than I can say for you*, I wanted to say but wisely refrained. "Anyone who knew Marion for more than a week knew she was one contrary woman. It's a miracle we worked together for the two years we did without me for real laying my hands on her. But I'd had it with her bossin' and told her so. She fired me in the same breath I told her I quit."

"Ah." Mark breathed the syllable. "So you're not going to be an easy one to work with."

"I'll do what you ask me to do, but don't go telling me how to cook this or that. Your menu needs some work, too. Serve something besides fried foods, and you'll double your business."

He looked amused. "Sounds like you want to be

both manager and cook."

"You just hear my opinions on matters, and we'll have our peace."

He laced his fingers and twiddled his thumbs. "Haven't had anyone else apply for the job." He stuck out his hand. "Welcome aboard, LaTisha."

I frowned at his outstretched fingers. "You hold on there. We've not talked money, and money is one of my favorite subjects, especially when it's my sweat earnin' it."

Mark's hand withered away. "I was planning on paying about eight dollars an hour."

"I ain't no young buck out of high school."

He ran a hand over his hair and down the back of his neck. "Well, how about eight-fifty?"

"I want eleven and an understanding."

"Eleven!"

"You won't be sorry if you hire my cookin'. A teenager, on the other hand. . ."

His chin dipped to his chest. "What's the understanding?"

I shifted forward and pitched my voice low. "Two dollars an hour of my salary goes to Tammy. If you tell her, I'll burn everything I cook. You feelin' me?"

"I'd just fire you."

Widening my eyes, I shook my head. "After all the people you'll attract with me as cook, you'd have a riot on your hands if you fired me."

"That's very generous of you. Uh, I mean about Tammy."

"She needs to get in school before her brain can't do backflips no more. I'm gonna get her there. Plus I'll have enough to cover my tuition."

"I'll make you a deal. If my business doubles within two months of hiring you, I'll give you a dollar-an-hour raise."

Spitting on my hand, I stuck it out. Mark blanched a bit but snuck his hand out. I slapped it loudly with mine and made sure to make real good palm contact.

"You can start tonight."

His hopeful expression almost made me laugh. "Nope, I need to talk to Hardy about this and get a good night's rest. There'll be a lot of preparation and rearranging of the menu before I ever set foot in that kitchen. How about next week? I'll come in tomorrow, and we can decide what dishes go and what stay." Scooting sideways like an overgrown fiddler crab, I hauled myself to my feet. Turning back to him, I pointed at the booth. "Those things need to go. Get yourself some decent seating."

"I'll consider it."

"Good."

Out of the corner of my eye, I caught movement. Valorie was headed in our direction. I had no doubt she would gain his full attention. "One more thing."

Mark raised his brows a notch.

"Does the name Jackson Hughes mean anything to you?"

"Sure, he was the assayer in our town legend." He turned, saw Valorie, and motioned her toward him, his expression concerned.

She smiled at me, and I grasped her hand, feeling her pain, seeing the tears forming in her eyes. "How are you, baby?"

She blinked, releasing a sluice of fresh tears.

Mark held his arms open to her, and she went willingly. "Shh. . .I'm here."

Muffled sniffles were the only sound until she leaned back in his embrace, wiping her eyes with the back of her hand. "Thanks, Dad."

13

Apparently it's no secret now." Hardy finished chopping the last of the squash and onions and pushed the cutting board at me. I swiped them into the pan and stirred them around. We'd both decided an early dinner would be better than a late meal, what with the council meeting and everything.

"Mark's a smart man. He knows what this is going to look like to the community. Here he is on the city council, and his—well, hmm, guess they weren't married. Anyway, she turns up dead, and he then admits that he is the long-lost father Marion was always complainin' about. Sure, people will think he has the perfect motive. Knowing Marion as everyone did, she wouldn't tolerate his interference in raising Valorie."

Getting to my feet, I stabbed at the two thick, breaded pork chops in the skillet. They smelled like heaven. Pink juices ran out of the holes I'd pierced. A few more minutes.

I rustled around in the drawer of pots and pans before I found a smaller skillet and set about frying a couple of pieces of bacon.

"Regina's patrons sure will be disappointed to know those hair clippings weren't the result of an evil mind," Hardy said.

"Quite clever, in my book, of him to think of such

a thing." I covered the bacon with a lid. "With studying the way they use DNA for such things nowadays, I'm a mite disappointed I didn't figure that out."

"You said you thought Mark looked familiar somehow when you talked with him. If you'd had more time, you would have figured out the similarities in their features, though Valorie favors Marion more."

"I sure hope so."

"What made you decide to work for him?"

Hardy's tone held something more than a note of surprise. I narrowed my eyes at him, trying to attach an emotion to the tone. "I'll need the money for tuition, and it'll give me a chance to be close to the townsfolk on a more regular basis."

"Stuck in a kitchen?"

"You don't mind it when I'm stuck in this kitchen."

"That's because I get to see you when you're here. I've gotten used to having you all to myself." His brown eyes were earnest.

I covered his hand with mine to take the sting from my words. "You know I got to work to pay for the college. Your retirement check isn't enough."

"I know that."

But he wouldn't look at me. I squeezed his fingers. "You missing the work?"

"No." His shoulders seemed to slump more than normal. "I enjoy getting up when I want to and doin' what I want to do, but without you here, and with Lela gone, it gets powerful lonesome."

I couldn't believe my ears. "So you askin' me to quit before I ever start?"

His shoulders lifted in a shrug. "Don't rightly know what I'm askin'. I know it's been your dream since you was a kid to have a degree. That's why I was so pleased when you married me instead. But it's been ticking inside you all these years to go back, so I want to see you do this, and our empty nest gives you the time to work on it." He picked up the knife and tapped the handle against the table. "I just didn't think retirement would be like this. I spent most my life raisin' up in the mornin' and hustling to work, then coming home to you and the babies. . . ."

I felt something give in my chest and went to him. *This* I could understand. And his admission warmed my heart. He didn't want me to leave him alone. "It's a new chapter in our lives."

"I know." He tilted his head to look up at me, brown eyes sincere. "It helped me to know you were feeling it, too. Until I talked to you the other night, I wasn't sure what it was gnawin' at me."

I pulled his head to my waist and stroked the grizzled gray and black head. He needed me, wanted me, and I didn't need to be forgetting that. Even if our babies were all gone, the good Lord had left me with a precious man to care for and love on. I didn't need to be making decisions without him.

My line of vision was pulled to the wall where the smiling faces of our children beamed down on us, the clock itself a silent reminder of time's passage. The harder I tried to keep up, the faster the seconds ticked. We'd be grandparents soon, but even still, our children lived too far away to visit often. Besides, they needed room to build a life for themselves.

My eyes roamed the kitchen as I opened my mind to the first suggestion that offered a doable solution. My gaze landed on the cutting board of chopped vegetables, and a lightbulb flashed on in my head.

"Hardy, honey, I do believe I have a solution to your dilemma."

Hardy affected his best formal pose and stoic face as he practiced his maître d' skills. I was playing the customer. Good practice for his new job as waiter. Yup. That's what we figured out between us. If I was to be away from home acting as chief cook, then he would hire on as a waiter.

"Good evening, ma'am. A table for two?"

I decided it best to put his staunch stoicism to the full test. "You suggesting I need two tables for myself? Can't you see it's only me?"

Unaffected, Hardy bowed his apology. "In that case, ma'am, a table for one with two chairs."

"If I could move quick, I'd box your ears, Mr. Martyr D'."

"Good for me you're well grounded."

Hmph! He was having way too much fun. "You'd best get back to being nice before I change my mind about helping you. Pretend the Blightmans are arriving for dinner."

Hardy cleared his throat and resumed his dignified position. "Good evening, Mr. and Mrs. Blightman. Will there be a table for two this evening, or are you expecting company?"

"That'll do. Not quite so formal, though. People want to think they're remembered."

"I used their names."

"Try again."

"Good evening, Hal and Beth. A table for two, or are you expecting company?"

"The Blightmans aren't Hal and Beth."

Hardy rolled his eyes. "I was making it up."

"How about something more homey? Act like they're one of your best friends."

Hardy rubbed his belly and grinned at the imaginary Blightmans. "I's hungry; let's eat." He gave me a cheeky grin. "That better?"

"Mark won't like it none."

Hardy covered his face with his hands, his words coming out garbled. "Don't you have someone else you can make crazy?"

I pushed myself to my feet and gave him the once-over. "It's time for you to visit Sasha and Livy and see what they can do for you."

His hands fell away from his face, his expression incredulous. "That's a woman's store!"

"There's a department for men in the back, and," I said, pointing with my eyes at his pants, "they don't have polyester. We need to get you in something where you not steppin' so high."

A notorious nonshopper, Hardy's idea of new clothes meant the thrift stores in the city, the section where everything was marked down because it was so out of date no one wanted to buy it. And even then I could only get him to go once a year, if I was lucky.

"You comin' with me, LaTisha. I ain't being left to the mercy of a white woman who dresses like a Care Bear."

I loved to mess with Hardy's comfort zone and knew full well making him go into a department store such as Sasha owned would supply him with something to grumble about for an entire week. "We'll aim to do it in the morning."

The phone started to ring. Hardy snapped up the cordless from the table by the recliner. "Sure, Valorie. She's right here."

I took the phone. Hardy motioned he was heading upstairs. "Valorie, honey, what can I do for you?"

"I meant to ask you this afternoon, Mrs. Barnhart, but it slipped my mind once you and Daddy got to talking. Would you be willing to sing at my mother's funeral?" She paused, and I heard the stress in her voice. "We thought you were probably the closest thing Mom had to a true friend."

I frowned at that sad testament to friendship. Our relationship had been one of mutual toleration. I needed a job, and though I didn't realize it at the time, Marion needed someone who could read and manage the store. Still. . . "I'll do it, baby. No need to worry your head about it."

"Rehearsal is Friday evening," Valorie said. "Can Hardy play for you?"

"Sure he can. And I've got me a favor to ask. Have the state police released your momma's store? I've got a box of books in there somewhere that I paid for, and I'd like to have them."

"Chief Conrad asked me to hold off on plans to do anything. My dad promised me he would take care of everything when the time came. I gave him the keys to Mom's—"

I heard the catch in Valorie's voice. Next thing I knew, Mark came on the phone.

"Sorry, LaTisha. I'm sure you understand. It's still hard for her to accept all the changes that have been thrown at her at once. You were asking about Marion's personal belongings?"

"No, not that. I have a box of books that I bought from her that morning. It's a donation to the school library, and I'd like to get in there and get them if I could."

"You'd have to run it by the chief. I need to get in there, too, so I can get an idea of how much there is to haul."

"Thank you. As I've already told Valorie, I'll be there Friday evening."

Officer Mac Simpson visibly cringed upon seeing me enter the police station. I felt the beginnings of a smile, then remembered Hardy's unhappiness with my shenanigans. The wind left my sails, and I vowed to be good.

"How do you do this afternoon, Officer Simpson?"

Hands flat on the top of his desk, he dipped his head. "Doing well, thank you. That was a mighty fine pie you brought over, Mrs. Barnhart. I appreciate it." He sat up straight in his chair. "Now what can I do for you this morning?"

"I was wondering about that box in Marion's shop. You said you'd leave a note for the chief about it, remember?"

"Uh, yes, I did—I mean, I do. He's been very busy, and he probably forgot."

"Oh, that's okay, sweetie, but I still need to ask him about it. Could you. . . ?" I gestured toward the phone.

Within minutes I was sitting across from the chief. Officer Simpson stood in the doorway, having escorted me back.

"Thank you, Mac. Would you get Mrs. Barnhart a cup of. . ." He raised his brows in question. "Tea? Coffee? Water?"

"Nothing for me, Chief."

With a silent nod, Conrad dismissed Simpson, and the door closed with a soft click. The chief's face, I noticed, held signs of fatigue. Lines that hadn't been there before Marion's death.

"This whole incident must be hard on you," I said, offering my sympathy.

"The state police are really pressuring me to let

them question people. I tried to tell them they could play tough guy if they wanted, but everyone would clam up pretty tight." He blinked slowly. "Guess I hail back to the days when cops played the good guys and didn't make threats and throw their weight around to get results. It's probably why I'm a small-town cop. I like the peace too much."

"I'm with you on that. Are they done tearing apart Marion's shop yet?"

"They stopped in yesterday and did a few more things. Since I'm so short-staffed, they offered to post a guard, but I told them I'd just hang a lock on the door until I heard back from them. Mark called this morning and explained his situation—you could have knocked me over with a feather when he told me he was Valorie's father. But what he really wants is to take a look at the inside of the store and get an idea of what he has to deal with when the time comes."

"I know. I talked to him last night. That was part of the reason I came today. You know about the donation the parents started for the school library? I bought some books from Marion that day. Only got one box out. So if you'll let me, I'd like to get the other and take it to the school."

"I don't know." Chief stretched backward and put his hands behind his head. "Guess it wouldn't hurt anything. I'll have you sign for the books." He stretched out his arm and yanked a key ring off the board behind his head and sat up. "We'll stop in at Mark's and see if he wants to go with us."

"There's something else, Chief."

Chief, halfway out of his seat, fell back into his chair.

"I got to talk with Regina yesterday."

He pulled a pad of paper close and jotted something, then leaned forward and clasped his hands together. "And?"

"I didn't get the conversation turned around to the campaign, but Sasha came in to have her hair done and rattled on about how it worked out so good that Regina canceled their Tuesday appointments, 'cause a shipment came in and it took them from ten o'clock until noon to get everything put away. Don't you think that's suspicious?"

"Did she give a reason that I could check out?"

"Said she had a long lunch date."

"I'll ask around a bit. Unless her date was at her house, Mark's is the only other place she could go. I wonder if she canceled all her afternoon appointments. Can you find that out?"

"I sure can try. I've got another appointment with her tomorrow; we're going to try out a new hairstyle. She was going to visit her momma today."

Chief stood, rounded his desk, and held out his hand to help me to my feet. Such a nice boy. "Makes me glad to have short hair."

As we walked toward the door, one other thing occurred to me. "I read in the paper that you guys were called to the scene of a supposed theft at Dana's house Monday evening before Marion's death. What's up with that?"

Chief hit the palm of his hand against his head.

"It seems Payton was the only other person in Dana Letzburg's house when an old diary of great personal value to her came up missing. She said he was there to tune her piano and was the only one who'd been inside."

We stepped into the sunshine together. I sucked in a deep breath of the fresh air. Fresh except for the pervasive scent of grease wafting down the street from Mark's place.

"What'd the boy have to say in his defense?"

"Payton?" Chief's brow creased in concentration. "He denied it, of course. Said he tuned the piano and left when he was finished. Even vowed that he locked the door."

I chewed on that a minute. If Payton tuned that piano, I was a bathing suit beauty. If I mentioned being at Dana's the same day after I found Marion's body because I'd figured out she was the person Marion was talking to on the phone, would Chief get angry with me? Getting arrested for obstruction of justice didn't seem a wise thing to do. "I visited with Dana that evening. She mentioned that diary to me. But I can tell you that piano wasn't tuned."

Conrad didn't seem interested. "It doesn't matter now anyhow. Dana left a message at the station really late Tuesday night saying she'd found it and thanking me for my help."

Since I didn't drive Old Lou that evening, Chief insisted we take the police car to pick up Mark at the restaurant. The squad car smelled unused and musty. Chief kept it clean, though, I'll give him that. Probably didn't have much mileage on it, either, since he only drove it on rare occasions, preferring to walk, as did most of the townspeople.

"It'll get everyone to talking if they see you in here," Chief said. "Could loosen the tongue of the guilty person if they think I'm zeroing in on you."

I sat in the back to make our little drama look more official. "Never had a chauffeur before. Makes me feel like Mrs. Eugene Taser acts. Speaking of which, can't you ask some well-placed questions of the mayor about. . ."

He put the car in reverse and twisted in his seat to back up. "About?"

I lifted a finger to indicate he should be quiet. "Just a minute. Something's brewin' in my brain." For sure it was! When Betsy told Regina to put it on her tab, I thought it strange since Regina has customers pay cash. Why would she allow Betsy Taser special treatment? I doubted she did it because she liked Betsy.

Chief parallel-parked in front of Your Goose Is Cooked. I wondered if the police had to fill the parking meter or not. He slid out and hunkered down until he could see me through the back window. "You stay put."

I lifted my hand as if to open the door, but there wasn't a handle. "Doesn't look like I'm going anywhere anyway." But that was fine with me. I had some more thinking to do.

Chief Conrad stopped to feed a coin into the meter before he disappeared into the shop. I rolled around the

Regina–Betsy Taser connection. Like a flapping moth, some important connection between the two kept eluding me. The mayor. . .scandal. . .money missing. . . Regina. . .her mother. . .

It rolled into my mind just as a burst of heartburn from my huge breakfast burned my stomach. It made sense. Testing the theory would prove tricky. If I was wrong, it could really crush Regina. I would need to exercise great caution.

Mark and the chief came out together, laughing over some inanity. When Mark started for the front seat, the chief stopped him and walked him around the car to the back door behind the driver's side. If they were playing to the supper crowd who had stopped to watch, they weren't doing a very good job by laughing the whole way to the car.

As Mark slid in, he gave me a rakish grin. "Howdy, fellow inmate."

I scowled. "You'd just best be stayin' on your side of this here car."

As the chief slid behind the wheel, Mark tapped on the wire cage separating the front seat from the back. "Can you turn the light on for real effect?"

"Already got a gang of people staring," the chief said as he waved at the small group gathered outside.

"Their curiosity is probably killing them."

"I'm glad Valorie isn't here. I'll have to explain before news gets to her that her father rode off in a police car."

Chief Conrad followed us into Out of Time. In the dim light from the front window, it took my eyes a minute to adjust. I raised my hand to flick on the light switch beside the door. Chill bumps raised along my arms.

A fine coating of fingerprint powder covered almost everything. Without Marion's strident voice to bring life to the store, it felt as though the bricks and boards themselves were grieved over what they had witnessed. Tendrils of musty air, coupled with a whiff of some unidentifiable chemical, swirled under my nose.

Mark's expression was unreadable as he stared around the shop. "She sure has a lot of stuff." His eyes darted to mine. "Had."

"You've never been in here before?"

His gaze fluttered away from mine. "Never."

Hmm.

Chief Conrad tucked his thumbs into his belt. "Let's get to what we came here for and get going."

So he feels it too. . . .

"Maybe this wasn't such a good idea," I murmured.

The chief squeezed past me in the narrow room. "Where would your books be?"

"The box I got was on the counter. Hardy took it out that day. Never did find the other one before I found her."

Chief peered up at the tall bookshelves then down at the floor. "Don't see any boxes here. Maybe behind the counter? Don't know where else it could be." He went to the end of the soda fountain counter and looked back at me. He must have sensed my reluctance. "Come on, LaTisha. It's okay."

My heart started to pound hard, and I took a deep, steadying breath to steel my nerves before I took the first step in that direction. But my mind wouldn't let me go farther than the counter. "You do the lookin' for me."

Chief's eyes creased at the corners, and he braced a hand on the counter as he bent to look behind it. "Bingo. There's a huge box here on the floor. Looks like they lifted some prints." He sucked in air and let loose, launching a cloud of fingerprint powder into the air. He hoisted the box onto his shoulder and headed for the door.

"You need more time, Mark?"

Mark had shimmied underneath the piano. "A few more minutes. This thing sure is old. It'll cost a bundle just to get it moved out."

"Maybe Payton'll take it off your hands," Chief offered.

Seeing that Mark's interest in the piano was minimal, I ran my fingers over a few of the ivory keys. "It's definitely out of tune. What does anyone know about John Broadwood pianos?" I asked no one in particular.

Mark scooted out into the aisle, stood up, and brushed off his knees. "There's a number under there.

Is there a pen and paper anywhere?"

"I've got some in the car—it'll give me a chance to put this box down, too." Chief maneuvered past me, toward the front door.

"With Hardy being such a natural, you've probably seen a lot of pianos. Know anything about how to identify one?"

"It's a Broadwood. They're made in England. What more do you need to know?"

"I was thinking more along the lines of the year it was made."

"Should be a serial number. Probably the one you saw underneath. Best way I know to identify these things is by the name." I folded my arms to squelch a shudder. Being in this store was worse than I thought it would be.

"Maybe I will have Payton come look it over." He raised the lid of the piano and propped it open with the stick. "Sure is dusty."

"If I had to guess, I'd say you'd get more for Marion's books than for that old piano. Hardy wouldn't touch the thing." In an effort to distract my imagination from the constant replay of Marion's body as I had found her, I ran my eyes along the books in the bookcase across the room. "If you give me a good price, I might try to buy these for the school library."

"The bookcases sure are huge. They don't look to be in bad shape, either." He rubbed his chin. "How about you pick out the ones you want, and I'll sell the rest?"

"My money's good."

"I don't doubt that. Consider it a donation to the donator, and Valorie won't care." He came to stand at the end of the dining room table that one had to skirt to get to the bookcase and raked his eyes over the spines of the various books. "Quite a few on local history. Maybe I'll take a couple to read to help with my article for the paper."

"They're your books."

His expression grew sad. "Actually, they're Valorie's. She inherits everything, as she should. She's a little reluctant to come here right now, though, so I offered to help clear things out."

Most of the titles were still easy to read, so I skimmed them, noting which ones would make good additions to the school's collection. It took me a few minutes to realize that Mark, though he held one of the two books he'd pulled out, wasn't reading at all. He seemed to be studying the bookcase itself, tracing it with his eyes. Probably trying to decide how much profit it would bring for Valorie. When he caught me staring at him, he snapped the book he held shut and placed it on the dining room table.

Chief came back in then. In his right hand, he clutched a pad of paper, which he slid across the dining table toward Mark.

I decided I'd had enough of the place and followed Mark. He took a minute to recheck the number and jot it down. We made it to the front door when Mark pivoted back toward the room. "Almost forgot my books."

Chief rattled his keys. "I'll unlock the car."

As much as I'd wanted to leave that shop, something made me stand right where I was and follow Mark with my eyes. He reached across the dining table and grabbed his books. Then he tucked them underneath his arm and paused. In profile, I could see his eyes lift toward the bookcase again. He put a hand down on the dining room table as if to rest his weight, but he must have pushed, because the table slid across the floor and butted up against the bookcase. One of the chairs fell backward with a thud, and the other one tilted and wedged itself underneath the lip of the bookcase.

"What's going on in here?" Chief asked as he came back inside.

Mark's gaze met mine. He pointed. "Guess the table wasn't as heavy as I thought. I leaned against it and it slid."

"Better leave it, then. The state police will be breathing down my neck if everything is messed up. Are you ready?"

Mark and I filed out to the car ahead of Chief. He stopped to secure the store.

"If you don't mind, Chief, I think I'll head out on foot. I need to get over to city hall for the council meeting." Mark paused, eyes shifting back toward the store. "Do you think I could get in there again with a piano mover to get an estimate?"

"You call me," was all Chief conceded. He held the front door open for me, and I fell onto the seat, glad to be off my feet.

I watched as Mark walked to the front of the hotel and turned the corner toward his restaurant, wondering about his little stunt in the shop. Something about his interest in that piano and those books and bookcase didn't ring quite true, but if someone asked me why, I wouldn't have any idea how to answer. It was just a feeling.

The citizens of Maple Gap put in a strong showing at the city council meeting on Marion's building. Councilman Lester Riley seemed pleased by the turnout, evidenced by the twinkle in his eye at every person who walked through the back door. Rumor had it that Lester was working to replace Eugene Taser as mayor in the next race. I'd vote for him. Lester's heart was in the right place, and his wife, Mary, would see no sense in puffing herself up like the current mayor's wife.

Dressed in his best—a clean pair of overalls—Lester greeted us as he would anyone: a howdy for me and a sound slap on the back for Hardy. I made sure to check out his boots, too. Never can tell when a farmer, especially a dairy farmer, might be carrying lethal cow patties on the bottoms of his boots. To my surprise, he had on fancy cowboy boots. Who'd have thought for a minute that he owned anything other than those galosh thingies he always wore, even around town?

I spied Payton sitting in the front row, still in monochromatic white. His expression matched his clothes. Made me wonder why this whole incident with Marion's building concerned him so much. It had certainly surprised everyone when he blocked Marion's sale by spouting arguments of the building's historical value. Secretly, I doubted the city council had been impressed by the arguments he'd presented two weeks ago. After all, building more houses equaled more taxable households for the city.

Other familiar faces lined the rows behind Payton, mostly older townsfolk who hated to see the building be torn down because they didn't like change.

I didn't like change, either, but I knew it was inevitable.

Shock ran along my nerves when I spotted Dana Letzburg. Slouched in a chair in the last row, her gray T-shirt and black jeans gave the impression that she wanted to disappear. When she caught me looking, she gave a wan smile, like that of someone recovering from a serious illness. It seemed fitting that she be present, somehow. The building had been part of the legend that had made the Letzburg name so well known.

Mark sat in his usual place with the rest of the council. Valorie sat with those citizens who supported the destruction of the building. She looked confident and fresh, though I figured the townspeople would be torn in their feelings about her. On one hand, she'd been caught cheating and branded untrustworthy as a result. On the other, her mother had just died, and most would feel it was noble of her to take up her mother's cause.

As Lester called the meeting to order, I found my seat. Hardy had slipped up to talk to Payton. He skedaddled back to me, his grin wide.

Lester began by allowing some of the citizens to speak on behalf of saving the building, citing historical reasons. Then the opposing side spoke. Valorie didn't say much. She really didn't have to. As soon as she hit the podium, the tears started.

"My mother needed the money and felt the town needed the new growth to survive since many of the children raised here move away shortly after graduating." She paused for a long beat and made good use of the wad of tissues in her hand. "I hope the city council will vote to fulfill my mother's dream for the town."

Short, sweet, and to the point. Payton didn't look up once during her entire talk. I think he knew he was going to lose the vote.

And he did.

The council voted four to one, minus Mark's vote, in favor of selling the building to the contracting company. Mark never breathed a word of explanation as to his recusal. Maybe it had something to do with his being a history buff. Or with the fact that his daughter now owned the building. But for that to be the case, Mark would have had to know that Marion would die, then get the news to the paper in time for it to be in the hands of Maple Gapites the next day.

Lester caught me before I left, pumped my hand, and asked me when I was going to run for city council. I laughed. He didn't.

Out of my peripheral vision, I caught Hardy

dashing away as I listened to Lester list the reasons I'd make a good councilwoman. Mark snuck by the crowd, sheltering Valorie from the people with a polite smile and forward momentum.

"You'd make a great councilwoman, LaTisha. Think on it," Lester encouraged me.

"Bureaucratic mumbo jumbo isn't my cup of tea. I even hate tea." From there, my mind split between the conversation with Lester and puzzlement over where Hardy had got off to.

It took me awhile to disentangle myself from Lester, but I managed, only after promising to think things over. The crowd had thinned considerably, but I didn't see Hardy's hiked drawers anywhere in the building.

Night air, warm with a cool breeze, sharpened my temper. That man had better not have taken off without me.

A low whisper of voices caught my attention as I descended the two steps to the curb. The voices were coming from behind a tall privet hedge. Neither sounded like Hardy. I continued down the sidewalk, curious enough to take a peek and see who it was and ask if they'd seen Hardy. I stopped cold when I glimpsed Hardy's body wedged between two of the bushes, his ear obviously cocked toward the conversation.

"What you doin' in there?"

He brought his finger to his lips and rolled his eyes. The voices stopped talking. He frowned at me.

How was I supposed to know he was eavesdropping? I thought he'd gone and lost his mind, pretending he was a shrub or something.

Hardy slipped out of the hedge and wagged his hands in front of him, hustling me toward our car. I moved as fast as I could, trying to shut my door as quietly as possible. Hardy hunkered down behind the steering wheel.

"I can't get down that low."

"Then sit there and act as if you're waiting on me," he said. "Let me know who comes out of that hedge."

We waited like that for about ten minutes before Payton slid out of the break in the bushes about ten feet farther up from where I'd found Hardy. He got into his car and left.

"Payton."

"Did he see you?"

I crossed my arms. "It's dark. Hard to see black skin in the dark."

"No one else?"

The words were barely out of his mouth when Dana popped out of the privet hedge opening, looked up and down the sidewalk, and made a beeline for her car.

"Dana," I said. "She's getting in her car right now."

Her headlights wiped a circle around us as she pulled out of her parking space.

Hardy unfolded himself from the floorboard. "As soon as the meeting was over, I saw Dana and Payton pass each other in the hall. Looked like they were giving each other some kind of signal, so I followed them. Not a bad piece of detective work, if I do say so."

"What'd you learn?"

He turned on the motor and flicked on the headlights. "Couldn't hear too much. Something about his shop and them getting together there after midnight to search."

"For what?"

His eyes glinted. "I think she said, 'We've got to get in there and find the diary.' "

Aha! "So she didn't find that diary like she told the chief." But what was so important about that little book?

"There's something else." Hardy dug around in the breast pocket of his seersucker shirt. "As Payton hightailed it out of that meeting, he slipped his wallet out and these fluttered to the ground."

These turned out to be a receipt from the dry cleaners and several stubs of lottery tickets. "He must be playing hard."

"Guess he's stopped terrorizing the fire-hall bingo regulars and expanded to the Lotto." Hardy whistled low.

My mind shifted from one thing to another. If Hardy'd overheard Payton say something to Dana about his apartment, I might think they had a thing for each other. But his shop?

As Hardy guided the car down Gold Street, I made up my mind.

"When you get home, I want you to change out of those beige pants and put on something black."

He looked at me as if I'd plucked my head bald. "What you thinkin', woman?"

"We're going to walk over to Payton's shop at

midnight. You and I are going to do a little spying."

I crossed my arms and huffed at the ceiling, where shuffling feet and an occasional thump let me know Hardy was hard at work getting changed. I'd hollered twice for him to hurry or our supper would be cold. I wanted to eat and get an assignment done before our spying session. With as little meat as he had on his bones, he should take less time than anyone to get dressed. At least he didn't have to tuck his excess into a pair of pantyhose. I could pin on a hat in less time than it took him to stick a leg into his drawers.

I determined I wouldn't waste another breath hollering. It didn't do any good. When the phone rang, I plucked it off its base and barked my greeting.

"Momma?"

Shayna. Funny, I should have been delighted, but in light of the other cancellations, I dreaded the call. Maybe she wanted to chat. After all, it had been awhile since I'd called her. If not for this investigation, I would have, since Thursday evenings are my normal night to reach out and touch my children. No matter what, after my talk with Hardy, I vowed I'd handle myself better if she called to back out of Easter dinner.

"It's about time you call your momma."

Shayna's laughter made me smile. "You must be waiting on Pop to get dressed. You have that edge to your voice."

That made me grin. How well they knew their

father and me. "You haven't heard the latest. Sit down and I'll fill your ear."

"Sounds serious." Her voice faded away for a second. She must have switched ears or something. "What's going on in Maple Gap?"

I inhaled, savoring that moment when I knew something someone else didn't. "I found Marion Peters deader than dead in her shop this past Tuesday."

"No!"

"Yes." I nodded as if she could see me, pleased at her reaction.

"What happened?"

"Not sure yet. With all the classes I've taken, I'm trying to piece things together. The state police did the forensics work, but you know how small-town people react to big-town folks. Marion's funeral is Saturday. You gonna come?"

"Uh, I'm thinkin' I'll be busy, Momma."

I closed my eyes. "We could sing together, like we did when you was young."

The other end of the conversation got quiet. "But I'm all grown up now. Didn't like singing then and still don't."

"You've got a beautiful voice, Shayna. You should use it."

"Actually. . ." She mumbled something.

"What you say?" The voice in the background at Shayna's sounded deep. Definitely male. "Is that Rhys I hear?"

"Sorry, Momma. Yeah, it's him. Anyway, what I called to tell you is important. Can Pop get on the other line?"

I reared my head back. "Hardy! You pick up that phone now, you hear? It's our baby."

"That's my ear you're yelling into, Momma."

"Sorry, honey. You heard from your brothers?"

"Talked to Tyrone last night. Cora's doing fine. She's had some Braxton-Hicks. Tyrone got real nervous."

A click on the line and Hardy's voice came on. "I'm here."

"Momma, Pop. . ." I steeled myself for whatever announcement was coming, reminding myself to play it down if she couldn't come to dinner. "Me and Rhys are getting married!"

As Hardy babbled his surprise and congratulations, my mind floated on another plane entirely. My remain-cool-at-all-costs promise didn't take in this kind of announcement. For sure! "You haven't been dating long enough to get married."

I didn't realize I'd said it out loud until I heard Hardy's tone. "Tisha."

"We've known each other a long time, Momma. I always admired him in college, and we took a course together. Worked on a project together for an entire semester."

"That's different than working on a lifetime together." I couldn't stop myself.

"Momma, he's a good man. Has a great job."

"You bringing him home for Easter supper?"

"Well. . ."

I refused to let the salt gathering in my eyes start spilling all over the floor. "Tell my son-in-law-to-be that I guess I'll see him at the wedding, then."

"We were thinking we'd go to the justice of the peace. You know. Small wedding, just the two of us. No fuss or frills."

Hardy was responding to her, but I couldn't take any more and slammed the phone down.

15

Hardy tried to bring up the subject of Shayna, but I stopped him, and neither of us had much to say for a long time. Hardy went to his piano and stayed there. I watched the clock closely and worked to finish my assignment on police procedure.

Finally, at eleven thirty, I put my books away and tapped Hardy on the shoulder. He kept playing. I pointed to my watch. He did a little grunt and stood up.

"I don't know why I agreed to do this." He fidgeted with the drawstring of his sweatpants, looking a little nervous. I didn't feel so good myself. *If we get caught. . .*

Erasing the idea from my brain, I smirked at him. "You look like a dipstick covered in oil."

Hardy grimaced at my choice of an old black knit outfit I'd found in the back of my closet. "And you look like ten pounds of potatoes shoved into a five-pound sack."

But the way his eyes glittered into mine let me know my stab at humor had helped lighten the mood.

We decided to walk. From our street, we turned onto Gold, then took a left onto Spender. As we neared Payton's store, we could make out a dim light coming from the back of the store. Passing Marion's shop gave me the shudders. Hardy must have sensed my distress, because he grabbed my hand and laced his fingers through mine. We looked for all the world like a couple out for a midnight stroll. Except two things.

One, Hardy and I were never up this late, and two, we were both dressed in black. Lucky for us the town's quiet streets meant everyone else had the good sense to be in bed.

We slowed our pace as we walked past Payton's store from the relative safety of the other side of the street. Definitely a light on in the back of the store. My heart raced at the prospect of discovering some secret, though I couldn't imagine what Payton and Dana could have in common that they needed to be together this late at night.

Hardy led the way around the building to the back, where a window in the back of Payton's store shone a patch of light onto the lawn. When we got to the window, we realized that even with my height, I wouldn't be able to see inside.

"Here." I motioned to Hardy. "Boost me up so I can see."

I glanced back at the window. Two more feet and I'd have a clear view. Hardy's cupped hands didn't appear, and I glared over at him.

"Uh, I was thinkin' about that ten-pound sack. Lookin' more like twenty all the time."

If looks could kill. . . But he was right. I cupped my hands and accepted his foot, boosting him high and locking my elbows.

For a long time, he didn't say anything. I was afraid to ask.

Finally, he motioned for me to lower him, but when I opened my mouth to ask what he saw, he put a finger to his lips and led the way back to the front of the store and across the road. He didn't speak until we got to Gold Street.

"They was together, all right."

"What were they doing?"

"They were in his office, looking at something that looked like a map of sorts. Couldn't see it clear-like. Dana didn't appear too happy with Payton, and Payton looked way nervous."

"That boy always looks nervous."

"Yeah, this time he looked *really* nervous."

I spent the trip home melting my brain trying to figure out what it all meant. I needed to find the connection between Dana and Payton. How I would go about it, though, remained a mystery.

I stroked Hardy's head where he had fallen asleep against my shoulder, thinking back over the day. Dana and Payton. Shayna.

Before sleep claimed him, Hardy had made sure to tell me something that shamed me deeply. "Shayna told me to tell you she loves you."

When I couldn't stand to stay on the line with my daughter another minute because Shayna's decisions didn't fit into my mold, my daughter blessed my name anyway. Rhys would be my son, not my son-in-law. He would be family. Problems would come and go between them, their love tested, but I vowed to offer encouragement when possible.

And the simple truth, the bottom line, was that

Shayna's life was her own.

Lord, it's taking me so long to learn to let go. My babies aren't my babies anymore. They never really were mine anyway, were they? I smiled into the darkness. *Here Tyrone's been gone for almost fourteen years. I should be used to the idea of them leaving. The leaving I can deal with; it's the not coming back that hurts.* A sob brewed deep in my heart, and I slipped out from under Hardy, not wanting to wake him by crying, I sat on the side of the bed and tried to put a plug in my emotions.

"Tisha?"

His hand tickled over my back. I never could resist his sympathy or his touch, and thank the Lord, I didn't need to.

"Spillin' tears again." I sniffed. "I didn't want to wake you."

"Listen, babe, I know you. You always come around. You've got a beautiful heart. But it's like I told you the other night—this is what you raised them to do."

"I know." My voice came out flat and emotionless. "God's showing me real good."

He pulled me back down beside him, cradling my head against his chest. Deep from his heart, straight to mine, came the words of "Leaning on the Everlasting Arms" in the raspy tenor I knew so well. He was a piano man, after all, not a singer. But the song poured sweetness over my soul and rocked me to sleep in the snug security of pure love.

16

Breakfast on Friday morning turned out to be a solemn occasion. Hardy, pouting about having to go to Sasha's, said little. He'd even worn a pair of decent navy blue pants, as if to prove he knew how to dress.

As I set his plate in front of him, complete with the chitlins I allowed him to have on occasion, his eyes pleaded with me. "You still makin' me go?"

"Yup." I fixed my own plate and sat down to join him. "After I've scandalized you by going into Sasha's, you can sit in Regina's while I get my hair done."

The whites of his eyes flashed.

"I'm getting a new style. Twist-outs."

"You already so twisted, I can't straighten you out."

He shoveled his food in fast. I picked at mine. "I've got to log on for my Friday morning class, shower, and then I'll be ready to go. Probably two hours. You can clean up for me."

"Need to work on planting seeds for the rest of the garden. You gonna help me put them out later this year?"

I grunted. "Don't I always help? Who you think stands here and chops up those vegetables and makes that salsa and cans that corn and okra and—"

"With putting out the plants."

"So long as you don't grow so much this year. I had so much corn last year, I thought I'd have to donate to the needy beaks of every chicken in the county."

"Hard to know how much to plant for two. Done so much planting for a big gang every year." Hardy scraped up the remains of his grits, slid the rest of the biscuit across his plate, and popped it into his mouth.

Something more than the size of his garden was wrong with him. "What's up your sleeve?"

He took his time chewing. "Been thinking about dogs."

"Dogs?"

"Chasin' their tails." He dabbed his mouth, the cloth napkin rasping against his whiskers. "They go 'round and 'round, and for no good reason. We're doing that."

"How you meanin'?"

"Maybe we're missing something in this thing with Marion. Do you think everyone you've questioned is a person of interest? Chief said your alibi was airtight. Was Payton's? Or Dana's? Or Mark's or Regina's?"

"You think Regina had something to do with Marion?" I thought about that lunch appointment she'd talked about.

Hardy raked his fingers over his face and rubbed his eyes. "Think on it, LaTisha. Even back when the campaign scandal broke loose, didn't half the town suspect that Regina's resignation had something to do with the money being gone? Only when Betsy's interview appeared in the paper, declaring Regina quit because of her mother, did things blow over."

My mind rolled over the conversation in Regina's shop. The woman's reaction when I mentioned Chief

Conrad's interest in the envelope. . . "You think Regina took the money and Betsy covered for her?"

"It's something to think on." Hardy stabbed at the chitlins. "Them's good eatin'."

His words barely registered. Didn't take a genius to know that Hardy's theory barked up the wrong tree. No way would Betsy Taser ever defend Regina. Especially over money meant for her husband. "Their relationship isn't a good one. Why would Betsy defend Regina?"

"Dunno."

My brain did backflips trying to recall the newspaper articles of that time.

Hardy's arm stretched toward the bowl of chitlins again. I batted it away. "They're not good for you."

"Then another helping of grits?"

As I fetched the grits for him and plopped them on his plate, a memory surfaced. "Who all was on that committee?"

"Not sure. Be a good thing for you to find out." Hardy's eyes squinted almost shut.

I picked up my dishcloth and ran it over the table as I thought it over. "I could ask Regina. Just come right out and drop the question."

"That's the way to do it." He skidded his chair back. "You sure you won't let me stay home this mornin'?"

Olivia Blightman's mother's store smelled like incense. Slender and blond, her figure ripe with youth, Olivia, or Livy as she preferred to be called, was known to be the kind of woman who tripped up a good man.

For a while, when Mark first came to town, he and Livy had been an item, their relationship heating toward critical. Rumors of marriage began to spread. I imagine Maple Gap women breathed a collective sigh of relief that Livy would no longer be on the prowl. Then she showed up at a community picnic solo, her eyes red from crying. Some speculated that the age difference had caused the split, Mark being forty-two to Livy's twenty-eight. She must have cared for him, though, because to my knowledge, she hadn't dated anyone else since, though Tom Spencer, owner of Grab-N-Go Gas, sure had tried.

Livy came toward us, sashaying through the racks of women's clothing like a runway model. Hardy started a melodramatic coughing fit as soon as he saw her. Maybe it was the incense. I opened the door and gave Hardy a good whack on the back with my other hand. "You get! Duck your head outside for a minute."

He slipped out the door and sucked in air, nostrils flaring with each breath.

"I'm sorry, Mrs. Barnhart." Livy's expression tightened with concern. "The air freshener my mother uses is a little heavy. After being here for so long, I got used to it."

I scanned her from tip to toe. "Smells like something illegal."

"I assure you it isn't."

I checked on Hardy, who was bent over but not coughing anymore.

I looked back at Livy. "We came to look at men's clothes. It stink back there, too?"

Livy looked unsure. "Probably not, since it's in a separate section."

"We'll go 'round back, then, and through that door."

"But it's locked."

I rolled my eyes. "Then I guess you'd best be unlocking it for us."

Not giving her a chance to protest, I stepped outside, slipped my arm around Hardy's shoulders, and guided him to the back of the store.

His thin shoulders still spasmed with light coughs, his eyes a little bloodshot from all the pressure. My hand traced light circles on his shoulder as I waited for the door to open.

"I'll be fine," he finally gasped.

"It was pretty thick in there. Wonder what that girl's burnin'. I can tell you Sasha wouldn't like it none to know her store is so full of smelly stuff that her customers almost choke to death."

"Do I have to go in?"

I patted his shoulder. "You sure do." The door cracked open, Livy's smile greeting us.

As if all the fetid air stopped at the doorway separating the men's shop from the women's, only a touch of the odor could be detected in the men's department. Mostly, the men's section smelled of leather and new carpet. Because Sasha received so few male customers, her selection was slim, but that didn't worry me any. Hardy wore common sizes. Had to laugh when I glimpsed his expression. His eyes trawled the room as if some terrible monster of the deep might pop up to eat him at any second.

Livy sashayed up to Hardy looking like a cat on the prowl with a dislocated hip. "I'm sure I can help you find something to make you look real nice, Mr. Barnhart. Style is my specialty, and with your unique physique, it shouldn't be too hard to—"

I stopped her forward progress with a loud whistle and a hard look. "His *unique physique* is my business, so how 'bout we just call you when we're done in here?"

Livy flinched. "That would be fine. I'll wait here while you all browse."

Ushering Hardy ahead of me, I went directly to a rack of short-sleeved shirts in bright colors.

"I ain't wearing purple, LaTisha."

"Nope, but a nice green and this here melon color would be right smart. Might even fill out your shoulders a bit."

He swelled up. "Nothin' wrong with my shoulders."

"Oh, baby." I scanned him with my eyes. "You are so right. You tuck underneath my arm perfectly."

I gathered three more shirts—passion blue, fire red, and lemon yellow.

"I ain't wearing yellow, either."

"You'll wear what I say you'll wear, because otherwise that little girl over there with the broken hip is going to dress you up in a suit and tie." I shoved the pile of shirts at him and turned him toward the dressing room. "Now get in that dressing room and try on those shirts while I look for some leather pants for you."

His eyes rolled, whites gleaming. "Leather!"

I patted his bum. "It'll all be over in about fifteen minutes. Be brave." Hardy gave me one more terrified glance before shutting the door to the dressing room.

Sasha breezed in about fifteen minutes later, looking spiffy and cool in a light pink sweater set and sea green capris with polka dots of the same color as the sweater. Another scarf, this one tied around her head, finished the outfit. I couldn't look that good if I had a whole closet full of cute clothes. Disgusting.

"How are you doing this bright, beautiful day, LaTisha?"

"Doing great. Got any leather?"

Grunting sounds of protest echoed out from the dressing room.

"Black ones," I added for Hardy's sake.

Sasha didn't miss a beat. "Sure. I have some. Not many, but we can find something for Hardy. Most guys want to get them to fit a little snug anyhow." She wagged her brows at me.

"And a jacket to match. With fringe."

"I'm almost done in here," Hardy said, the door garbling his words. "Then we can get out of here. Don't need no leather anyhow. What you thinkin'?"

I spun around and zeroed right in on the two racks of men's pants—solid color, all cotton. It meant more ironing, but Hardy's love of crisp pleats would terminate my position as iron wielder very quickly. He always did a much better job.

Grabbing his size in every color, I slung them over the door. "You try these on, too, you hear?"

Another grunt.

Sasha and I shared a conspiratorial grin. She crooked her finger at me, and I followed her through the cloud of stinky air to the front of the store. The little hat still sat on the mannequin's head in the window. With an easy motion, she jumped up into the window, took the hat off the figure, and handed it down to me.

Even with my twists still in, the hat perched perfectly on my head. "I'll take it."

"Thought you might." Sasha hopped down from the ledge and glanced at the price tag. "I'll give you 25 percent off."

"Sweeten the deal any more and I'll buy two."

Scanning the tag, Sasha punched some keys when it beeped a protest. "This thing can be such a pain. And I do have one in yellow if you're interested."

"Lemon yellow?"

Her head cocked to the side. "Pale yellow."

"Naw. Not my color at all." I glanced over the bald-headed mannequin and out the window to the street. "Regina's doing quite the business today. She's getting me a new hairstyle." I touched one of my twisted rows of hair. "I'm done with relaxers."

In an unconscious gesture, Sasha touched her hair. "Makes me glad I just need a trim every now and again."

From the doorway to the back room behind the cash register, Olivia appeared, rubbing her hands together then running them over her pant legs.

"Back there snacking?" Sasha asked as she wrapped my hat in tissue paper. Olivia crouched and took out a flattened box, punching it and shaping it into a square large enough for my hat.

"Carrots. Seeing Regina flip her sign reminded my stomach to start rumbling."

I glanced over at the beauty shop and saw the WILL BE BACK sign on Regina's door. When the door swung inward and Regina appeared, Sasha laughed out loud. "She must know we're talking about her."

But my mind zeroed in on Regina. Tucked under her right arm, she carried a white envelope. What was that gal up to?

As Sasha wrapped my hat in the tissue paper nest Olivia had made for it, Olivia said something that caused my heart to drop to my feet. "Wonder what she's up to. That's the second time this week she's clutched that envelope to her chest like a newborn. Must be sending something to her mother in Denver."

—

"I feel like a starch can," Hardy grumped. His pants swooshed with every step. "And I can't believe you made me get a suit. What do I need a suit for? I don't work anymore."

"It was the suit or the leather. You made the choice."

"I chose the leather." He opened the back door of

the car and let the bags spill onto the seat.

"Only because Livy whistled. The suit was life, the leather death."

His eyes twinkled. "Suppose I'd like to live to see my grandbaby."

"My feelings exactly. You've got the suit. Breathe and enjoy."

One package fell to the ground. He picked it up and crammed it in with the others.

I watched his hind end wag around as he arranged the packages. "Why don't you put all that in the trunk?"

"No need; I got them all in. Besides, those books are still in the trunk."

The box of books. In all the bustle, I'd forgotten about them and about the box still in Chief's trunk.

Hardy gave a mighty shove of the bags, backed out of the way, and slammed the back door quickly. "See?"

Hardy and I crossed the street to Regina's, him swooshing the whole way. Regina's shop displayed the OPEN sign again. "I'm needing to go to the police station and check in with Chief."

"You go on ahead." He pointed with his thumb. "I'll sit in here and wait for you."

Now, I could have warned him about the pre-weekend crowd. The majority of womenfolk got their hair done on Fridays so they could look nice all weekend, especially for Sunday. If he wanted to sit with a roomful of gossiping women, let him, I had fifty minutes before my hair appointment and needed to find out if Regina's alibi checked out.

Sunshine made it a pleasant walk, and a new pair of hose made it bearable.

"Good morning, LaTisha." Chief greeted me from a desk covered with everything from potato chip bags to a bottle of toilet cleaner. I made a point of staring at the desk with raised brows. Chief chuckled. "I'm also janitor of this place." He motioned to the toilet cleaner. "Guess I got distracted, and instead of putting it away, I carried it out here. Mac's a lot neater, huh?"

"No doubt you have a lot on your mind." I lowered myself into the nearest chair. "I need to get that box of books out of your trunk. I'll send Hardy over to get it."

"Sure." Chief nodded, brows pinched together. "I received the results from the fingerprint test. Regina's prints were all over that envelope. A partial shoeprint didn't yield anything other than it was a woman's shoe." He released a sigh. "Which isn't unusual being it was a store."

"No other test results?"

"They took several samples of other items, but Officer Cameron said everything got pushed aside when three other murders took place Tuesday afternoon, so they're backed up. I'm going to try to make a trip over there to get things stirred up."

"Have you questioned her?"

"Regina? Not yet. With her mom not doing well and all. . .well, I haven't talked to her." His fingers began a dance on the surface of the desk. "I was hoping you could do that for me. She might open up more to you than she would me."

His dancing fingers had my brain jumping in time. This boy was nervous. Agitated. Something had happened to make him so shy. I intended to find out what that something was.

He had slicked back his hair today, taming its normal tousled appearance. As his fingers bounced, a suspicion bloomed in my head. Regina Rogane probably was about the same age as the chief.

"You thinking 'bout courting Regina or something?"

Never in my life had I seen a white man blush so hard. His face flushed so red I thought he might be holding his breath. He sat up a little straighter and crumpled the potato chip bag, tossing it toward the trash can, then began clearing his desk of everything as if his life's work were to compete against Mr. Clean. "She's a nice lady," is all he offered.

Now, I'd seen this before. RBCD is what I call it— rapid brain cell depletion. It's the disease that affects every man and woman in the throes of "like," "love," whatever. They start acting as if all the sense they ever had was the pennies in their pocket.

Chief's long fingers made short work of the rest of the garbage, until only the toilet bowl cleaner remained. He stared at it before finally raising beseeching eyes to me.

"What do I do?"

"Cupid I'm not, honey. You gonna have to work this thing out yourself."

"I feel like such a fool walking in there and questioning her on Marion's death. Regina wouldn't do such a thing. I know she wouldn't."

I crossed my arms. "You crushing hard, boy. But you got a job to do. She know how you feel?"

Another wave of red boiled his ears. He shifted in his seat. "No. I don't know if she's. . ."

"You'd best be finding out, don't you think?"

His eyes went huge. "I can't come right out and ask her. Not now."

"How else you thinking you going to find out? Osmosis? And how is it you know her momma's not doing well?

"I was eating at Mark's the other night, and she was talking to Tammy. You know, girl-talk type of stuff. Tammy has a new boyfriend. Then Regina started crying and I heard her say something about Denver, so I figured it had to do with her mother."

"Well, you don't worry your head. I'm guessin' we'll cover a lot of territory while she gives me my new hairstyle." I touched my hair and gave an affirming nod. "Lots of territory."

"And, LaTisha. . ." His fingers stopped tapping on the surface, his stare unwavering. "I'd appreciate it if you wouldn't let on about me. . .you know."

"My lips is sealed."

17

With a good thirty minutes left before my appointment, I ducked in at Regina's to tell Hardy to get the box out of Chief's trunk, then went over to the school to let the librarian know the books were coming. I also hoped for a chance to see Dana in action, maybe even talk to her.

I did my best to move fast to get over to the school while most of the kids would be eating lunch. Some of the little ones were headed in from recess. If I'd have had a red flag, I'd have waved it at the charging group of youngsters coming at me down the concrete walk, yelling their greetings to me as they galloped past into the school. Behind them, I spied another familiar face.

"Howdy, Mrs. Barnhart." Teddy Cooper waved as he came even with me. A former Sunday school student, he was now a twelfth grader ready to take on the world. Scary.

"You just getting to school today?"

"No. I had a doctor's appointment."

"Well then, how you been? You gonna miss playing ball at that fancy college?"

Teddy played forward on the basketball team and had for four years. Known for his speed, he'd done his share of damage on visiting teams during the season.

"Naw, Mrs. B." Teddy shook his head. "I'm done playing ball. I've gotta really hit the books hard. Won't have time for sports."

As we passed through the doors and headed toward the centrally located library of the school, Teddy chatted on about his plans for a degree in computer science.

The green double doors of the library opened as we neared, and Sam Lightner, sloppy jock and proud of it, appeared, his shoulders slumped in perpetual bad posture, his pants riding low, ripped and torn.

Sam lifted his head, and his eyes flickered from me to Teddy, lingering on the boy a few seconds longer than necessary. Neither said a word. Sam looked away and kept walking.

"What was that all about?" I ventured.

Teddy didn't answer me. We watched Sam enter room 10. Dana Letzburg's room. "Good," I said, pleased. Dana must be alone during lunchtime for the older students. "Guess that boy's getting some extra tutoring."

Teddy turned his gaze on me. "It isn't tutoring that got him through Ms. Letzburg's English class. Uh—" He compressed his lips and turned his head away. "I shouldn't have said that."

Now, I haven't raised kids for nothing. Guilt, in its many forms, is a universal emotion betrayed by sudden stutters in dialogue and quick stops in speech. Then there's the way the eyes dart around or fasten on an object.

"If there's anything happening that shouldn't be, don't you think it should be known? Is that why Sam was sending you those silent daggers a few minutes ago?"

Teddy wiped the hair off his forehead. "I don't want to get anyone in trouble."

"Seems to me I taught you about honesty in Sunday school."

He slumped. "Guess it doesn't matter now that we're getting ready to graduate. With Ms. Letzburg catching Valorie cheating and all—"

"Did you know Valorie was cheating?"

He shrugged but didn't meet my eyes. "We went out a couple of times. She hated English. Who doesn't? We studied together for this really hard test. She got an A. I still got a C."

"If you studied, why was that such a surprise?"

I didn't miss the scarlet streaks that sprouted up his neck. He ducked his head even lower. And having been privy to the raging hormones of youth seven times over, understanding dawned.

"So you knew she'd cheated."

"Yeah, I guessed. I broke up with her after that."

"What's this have to do with Sam?"

"Kind of a double-standard thing going. Ms. Letzburg catches Dana cheating, yet the entire basketball team knows that she sells grades. That's what Sam's doing now. He got an F on a test on diagramming sentences that was a big portion of our grade."

My eyes were drawn to the doorway of room 10. I wanted to have a look. "You're awful brave to let this be known."

His chest rose as he straightened. "You're going to tell, aren't you?"

I nodded. "Think it's only right, don't you? It takes a bigger man to tell the truth than to lie."

Teddy shrugged, but I saw the relief in his expression. "Better coming from you than from me."

I grinned and patted his shoulder. "Let me go lay my eyes on the goings-on in that room. You scram on out of here."

When he disappeared from sight, I edged down the hallway toward Dana's room, checking through the windows of the classrooms as I passed, all of them empty except for two teachers deep in conversation in one and a teacher replacing books on a shelf in another.

Teddy's revelation disgusted me. How could Dana do such a thing? If there's one thing I value, it's a good education. Considering Dana was in a career designed to help young people be the best they can be, I found her deed sickening.

I stopped at room 10, right before I got to the window. Some sixth sense demanded caution. I peeked around the edge of the window that gave a clear view of room 10 and the people within.

Dana sat at her desk, her fingers dancing on the desktop. Sam stood in front of the desk, his wallet open. Though I couldn't hear her, she waved the wallet away and favored Sam with a serious expression. Her pencil hovered over the grade book a second before she erased a spot and wrote something.

A huge grin split Sam's face.

Dana dug around in her desk and slipped an envelope across its surface toward Sam. He took it and tucked it away in one of the many pockets in his jeans before turning toward the door.

I jerked back, turned, and hustled myself down that hall as fast as my legs could go. It didn't take me long to let the librarian know about the donation she had coming; then I hightailed it out of the school and down the road to Regina's.

I landed in Wig Out amid a flow of babble, a few minutes late for my appointment. No biggie. She had herself a full house anyway.

"Men are the worst."

Lynn Crawford, resident loudmouth, had a whole bunch to say, and she wasn't squeamish about talking loudly from her perch underneath the hair dryer. "Worse than babies, Madge—when they're sick you might as well shut the house down. You're not going to get anything done with them laying out in the middle of the living room moaning and groaning about how awful they feel."

"Yeah."

Then all eyes in the shop landed on Hardy, who slid even lower in his seat. The flash of sunlight on the door as it closed behind me dragged the attention away from Hardy to me. By the look of things, if I hadn't come in when I did, another group glare might have had Hardy dripping right out onto the floor.

He jolted upright when he saw me and pleaded with his eyes for rescue.

"You all ganging up on my man?" I smiled my words at the three women—Regina was noticeably absent from the group. Madge Kendry and Debra Zoe, along with Lynn, laughed.

"You came in the nick of time," Madge said. "We had Hardy on the hot seat."

Poor Hardy. Sometimes Madge brought her husband with her, and only with Nick present would Hardy usually enter the salon. Served him right for coming in here without me.

Debra swept back her overly long bangs. "Regina said you were up for a new style. What are you going to have done?"

I ambled over to the chair next to Hardy and patted his knee as I sat down. "Gonna have my twists taken out. She's gonna show me what to do. Wanted microbreads, but I'm not sure I'm up to handling all that hair."

"Shayna sure looked good in them," Madge said from her perch in Regina's chair, pink cape in place, one side of her black hair trimmed, the other side untouched. She jerked her chin to indicate the back room. "Regina got a phone call. She was saying she was already behind."

"I'm only due for a trim," Debra spoke up. "Lynn just needs a brush-out."

"I'm powerful hungry," Hardy whispered in my ear. "You gonna make me stay here the whole time? I've suffered enough."

"You be still and wait. If Regina's thinking it'll be

too long, I'll reschedule."

Madge leaned forward to make eye contact with Hardy. "Nick's over at Mark's if you want to wait for LaTisha there."

Hardy shifted closer, his breath warm against my ear. "Oh, they's all sugar and sweet cream to me now. Why didn't you tell me how much they love to torment?"

"Why didn't you just wait for me? And don't even think about moving out of that chair. You twitch and I'll strip off my pantyhose and tie you there."

A soft gasp made me turn. All eyes were on the doorway of the back room, where Regina stood, eyes puffy and red. Lynn turned off the hair dryer. Regina wiped moisture from her cheeks. "I'm sorry, ladies, I have to close shop." Her voice caught, and she cleared her throat on a sob. "Momma's taken a turn for the worse. I need to get there."

My heart churned in agony for the young woman.

Lynn slid the dryer into the upright position and began to pluck pins from her hair. "I'll give myself a comb-out, Regina. You go on and get on the road."

"And I can reschedule," Debra offered as she crossed the room to embrace the younger woman. "I lost my own mother three months ago. You'll let us know if there's anything we can do?"

Regina nodded.

Lynn tossed the curlers into the bin Regina used and the pins into a drawer. She sent Regina an air kiss and left.

The rip of Velcro signaled Madge's emancipation.

"There's worse than going around looking like a before-and-after ad." She touched Regina's shoulder. "Send Eloise our love, okay?"

By now, Regina's tears had started to flow again. My mind ran the gamut, from disappointment over not being allowed to ask her questions, to concern for the girl, to the chief's affection for the young woman. . .

The chief.

A plan formed in my mind as I grabbed Hardy's hand and tugged him to his feet. "You come with us, Regina. We'll get you over to your momma's real fast—the chief will make sure of that."

Only one thing almost quashed my ultimate plan to give Regina a chance to have some time with Chief Conrad.

Hardy.

We walked to the station, and I went inside to explain the situation. It didn't take much to convince the chief that now was a good time for him to go into Denver and check in with the state police. He could drop Regina off en route—since she was in no condition to drive herself anyhow. The chief acted like a small boy who had just bought his first puppy. But when I followed him outside, Hardy stood at the passenger's side door of the officer's personal car (white with lots of antennas). I sent Hardy eye-daggers and kept jerking my head to one side in hopes he would get the idea.

Chief blocked me from view as he greeted Regina

and said something that reduced his tough-cop persona to that of Silly Putty. I stepped around Chief's back and gave Hardy another head-jerk direction. He narrowed his eyes at me and looked concerned.

"Honey, you okay?"

Whatever drivel the chief had been driveling, both he and Regina turned their attention to me. I took a step back and grinned broadly at them. "No, sweetie, just needing to talk to you a bit. Privately. *In the backseat.*"

Hardy swelled up like a bloated toad and winked at the chief. "Woman can't get enough of me. Guess I'd better sit in the back."

As smooth as butter, Chief gestured Regina toward the passenger side and pulled open the door.

I slung open the back door, spread my hand on Hardy's head, and squashed him onto the seat. "You're so right, baby. You look so fine, I'm out of my mind."

I slammed the door as Hardy murmured, "Amen."

I rounded the back of the car as Chief went around the front. Our eyes met.

"Now play this thing smooth," I counseled. "How 'bout you let me ask the questions."

"Do you think it's a good time? Maybe we should wait."

I shook my head. "Leave it to me."

His Adam's apple bobbed, and he ducked into the car.

Regina remained quiet the first thirty minutes, and I allowed her the time to regain her composure.

My blood thrilled when I heard chief whisper across to Regina, "You okay? Your mother's a lucky woman. You've cared for her with more loyalty than most kids would care for their parents."

Regina sniffed, her profile showing the trembling of her lower lip. "She's all I've got."

I sat forward in the roomy car and patted her shoulder. "You've got a town full of people who love you and want what's best for you. You'll feel alone in your grief, but you won't be alone in spirit."

A tear trickled down Regina's face as she edged sideways in her seat. A small smile curved her lips. "I really appreciate what a comfort you are to people, LaTisha. To me. You always make me smile."

"She just makes me tired," Hardy piped up from the backseat.

I cuffed him on his arm. "You keep your trap shut. Can't say nothing nice, keep quiet."

But it was too late. Chief chuckled and Regina smothered a laugh. Before I knew what was happening, Hardy joined in. A chuckle rose in my throat. "You all make me crazy."

"Sorry, LaTisha, but you and Hardy are quite the couple." Chief's eyes smiled at me in the rearview mirror.

I slid my gaze over to Hardy. He flashed his gold tooth and winked. "Loving her for thirty-eight years. Every man should have himself a good woman."

Chief sent Regina a guarded look, half hope, half begging. She didn't seem to notice.

I struggled with how to get the conversation back

on track so I could dump some questions on Regina.

"I wonder how it was between Marion and Mark. You have any ideas, Regina?"

"She complained about Valorie's father a lot. She never said it was Mark, though it explains why she avoided him. They never married, you know."

"Didn't he come to town about the time you were involved in the mayoral campaign?"

Regina clasped her hands in her lap. "No, not that I can recall. He came later on."

Chief met my gaze in the rearview mirror, pure torture in his eyes. "That was always a mystery to me— uh, I mean, what happened during that campaign and everything."

"You'd think that money would have turned up somewhere," I added, flashing him an encouraging smile. "Guess whoever did it must have paid it back. That's the only reason I can think the mayor might have dropped the whole incident like he did."

"LaTisha and I were trying to remember just the other night who all was on that committee. Do you remember, Regina?" Hardy offered. "Wasn't Marion on it? You think she stole the money?"

I watched to see how my next words affected Regina. "Probably won't ever know. What do you think, Chief?"

"As a citizen. . ." He stuttered to a halt, and his eyes darted to mine again. He cleared his throat. "Someone on the committee had to do it." He turned his head to Regina. "You were involved in that campaign—what's your take on it?"

She didn't make eye contact with him. If I didn't know better, I'd have thought the woman was praying. My breath halted.

"Marion and I worked together. We weren't really good friends." She raised her eyes and caught Chief's gaze, then glanced at me. Something snapped in the brown depths of her eyes. A knowingness. A cautious flicker that said, *I don't know if I can trust you.*

"I don't think Marion knew quite how to love, but we're your friends, Regina." Whatever prompted me to say that?

Regina faced forward again, eyes staring out the front windshield. Her sigh whispered through the car, and Chief took one hand from the steering wheel and reached for Regina's hand.

"It's all in the past, Regina," I said.

She nodded. "You all know, don't you?"

"We guessed," I said in a low, soothing voice. "What we don't understand is that envelope you left on the counter at Marion's shop."

"I didn't kill Marion, Chief." The knuckles of her hand holding his turned white. "You've got to believe me."

18

As we rode along, Regina shared the whole story of the campaign funds. With composure and sadness, she explained how her mother's failing health had scared her.

"I knew Mother's sickness was getting beyond my ability to care for her. I had to get her in a home, and fast, but I didn't have a lot of money, and I hated the thought of putting her in the state's answer to those too poor to afford alternatives. So I—" She sucked in a breath. "I directed some funds away from the campaign." For the first time, she looked up, directly at the chief. "I fully planned on paying them back. I made that promise to myself."

"But Marion discovered your secret," I guessed.

Regina nodded, obviously miserable. "She threatened me. Called me a thief, and I guess I was, but I still knew I would pay them back. I told her that."

"That was over two years ago. Did you get caught up?"

"Yes. Three months ago. From day one, Marion agreed to keep quiet about it."

"That is strange," I said.

"Until last week. Then I understood her motive."

I figured I knew what was coming, and it sounded just like Marion.

"Last week Marion sent me a letter. She threatened to tell everything, but she'd keep quiet if I paid her three hundred dollars."

"The envelope of money was your payment."

Chief voiced exactly what I'd been thinking. "Your fingerprints were all over it."

"Yes, I knew you'd find that out. She came into my shop that morning and told me payment was due by noon." Her gaze swung to me, and she looked guilty and sad. "That's why I had to cancel those appointments. It wasn't a lunch date like I said."

"I knew that, baby."

"It really shook me up when she demanded the money that soon, and I knew she'd tell. I was afraid the whole town would blacklist me and I'd lose all my business. I worked myself up into a rage as I walked over to her store, and by the time I went in, I didn't care that she wasn't there. I slapped the envelope down on that counter and left." With her free hand, Regina wound a clump of hair around her finger. "You believe me, don't you, Chad?"

Again, I met Chief's eyes in the mirror and saw his distress.

"I believe you." Hardy sent his encouragement.

"I believe you, too," I added, "but your fingerprints being all over that envelope, and all that you just told us, really makes your motive rock-n-roll."

Chief, eyes on the road, let go of her hand. I felt for him mightily. He must be torn up inside big-time. His words, though, came out hard, coplike. "I need to think about this. I want to believe you, Regina. Really. But the cop in me says I'd better be careful. I can't afford a scandal, and this, unfortunately, makes you a prime suspect."

"I understand, Chad; it was your duty." Regina, head bowed, rubbed her thumb against her fingertips, as if trying to remove any last traces of the fingerprinting ink.

Because he knew he had to do it, Chief had taken Regina by the state police office and had her fingerprinted. He looked like a whipped puppy during the entire process, but knowing Regina needed to get to her mother, he tried to hasten the process along as much as lay within his power, promising he'd return later to discover what the state police had come up with on the case.

We left the station and went directly to her motel, where Regina handed me the key to her shop. Chief sat in the car, talking to Hardy. "You got clothes?" I asked.

She patted her purse. "I've got a little cash. I can always buy an extra outfit."

"I'll call and cancel your appointments for tomorrow," I assured her. "And Hardy can come haul you back to Maple Gap whenever you need. Just give us a holler."

She nodded and opened the door to her room. I reached to pull her close. Hated leaving her alone. Made me want to dig an elbow into Chief's side and tell that boy to get his act together and ask her out. Everyone needed someone, and Regina and Chief needed each other. But her confession had changed everything, and I also understood the chief's responsibility to do things by the book.

I patted her cheek and went back to the car, slipping into the front seat. "It's awful hard to leave her like this," I said as we pulled out of the parking lot.

Chief startled at my words, as though I'd verbalized his very thoughts, and judging by his hangdog look, I probably had.

I slipped off my shoes and rubbed my feet together. "My bunions tell me she's a good girl."

Tendons jumped in the chief's hands as he gripped the steering wheel. "I had to do what I had to do."

"Yes, but just because she admitted being involved in a scandal back then doesn't mean she killed Marion. Besides, there's something Hardy and I need to tell you about Dana and Payton."

Chief sent me a sideways glance then put his eyes back on the road. "Shoot."

"After the council meeting, Hardy overheard Payton and Dana talking. He picked up on a couple of things that made us think we should hustle on over there and see if we could learn anything. And he heard Dana say how they needed to find the diary." I hesitated to say that we spied. Unfortunately, Hardy had no such reservations.

He leaned forward from the backseat. " 'Bout killed LaTisha to have to hoist me up to the window so I could see into Payton's shop, but there was no way I could hoist her—"

I shot him daggers.

He got the message. "So's I saw them through the window. Payton looked all scared. Dana seemed angry. They was looking over some sort of drawing on a paper. Told LaTisha it looked like a map."

I leaned forward. "Maybe it's time we start looking

closer at Payton's and Dana's motives. And don't forget Mark. I need to have another talk with him. From that first day after I found Marion, I thought there was something Valorie wasn't saying."

Chief held the wheel with one hand and ran the other over his hair and down his neck. "Mark has a strong motive if Marion was prepared to give him a hard time about custody of Valorie. Payton's alibi is he was in his music store, and Hardy can vouch for that."

"Hardy can vouch for him being there a few minutes before we discovered her body, but nothing before that. What about Dana and that connection? Why would she point to Payton as a suspect for stealing her diary—"

Chief arched a brow at me. "I don't recall telling you it was over a diary."

For once, my brain froze over and I couldn't think fast enough to formulate a good evasive answer. "You didn't," I confessed. "Dana was the person on the other end of the phone conversation that I told you Marion was having when I was in the store before her death."

Chief's eyes crinkled at the corners. "In other words, you took it upon yourself to investigate before I asked you to help me out."

"You never asked me if I knew who Marion was talking to," I said, defending myself.

"Still, you shouldn't have taken it upon yourself. I have checked out her alibi at the school. Everyone there said Dana was in her classes and they saw her at lunch, but she came in late."

"But she's right across the street." I made a

whooshing motion with my hands. "It wouldn't take but ten minutes for her to dash across and do the deed."

"Motive?"

"She accused Valorie of cheating. Marion wasn't happy; I can tell you that."

"But that gives Marion more of a motive to knock off Dana."

I sat up straight. "They fought over a diary, Dana told me. Is it the same one she reported missing? If so, how did Marion get it, and why did Dana accuse Payton of taking it?"

"Why would Dana push Marion over a diary?"

"Dunno." I shrugged. "It's seeming like that might be important. If it's the same book she's looking for, it'd be good if we could find it first."

"Looks like we might need to go back and ask Dana a few more questions. I was over at the school today and saw her in class, alone with this kid. Looked an awful lot like they were up to no good. The kid pulled out his wallet. She refused it but erased something in her grade book and penciled something else in. Rumor is she's selling grades."

"I need some rock-solid evidence. I can't prove anything based on what you saw, LaTisha."

"I know." And that's what troubled me.

Chief pulled up in front of the precinct and glanced between Hardy and me. "You all want to come in?"

Hardy, his stomach always first priority, spotted a fast-food restaurant. "How 'bout LaTisha and I go pick us up something to eat while you go wheel and deal with the big-city cops?"

Chief leaned to one side, his hand traveling to his wallet.

"Nope. This one is on us," I said. "Just tell Hardy what you want."

He thanked us, and we all tumbled out. We expected it to take him a long time, but when we got back to the car, he sat inside, the music blaring.

"He don't look none too happy," Hardy whispered near my ear.

I flung open the front door as Chief fumbled for the volume and the music faded to a dull thump. Hardy passed the food around.

"No success?" I ventured before sinking my teeth into a nice greasy cheeseburger with everything on it except lettuce. Hate lettuce on my burgers.

Chief Conrad's head sank back against the headrest as he chewed. "Not yet. They said the tests would definitely be completed by Monday."

Secretly, I relaxed a bit, not realizing how tense I'd been at the thought that the state police might move in and take over the whole investigation based on their test results. I had the entire weekend ahead of me to do more investigating, or in my case, inguesstigating.

Tonight I needed to be at the rehearsal.

And tomorrow was the funeral.

"Can we talk more after this rehearsal's over?" I asked.

Chief nodded. "You know where to find me."

19

Chief dropped us off at Regina's. We hopped into Old Lou and rode to the rehearsal in near silence as I heard voices from long ago—the chatter of my babies as I hauled them to school or picked them up from a bake sale or from a fall carnival. Their little bodies would smell of sweets and fresh air.

Saturday mornings meant trips to the bakery on Gold Street that specialized in hometown goodness. The children would each get a free cookie of their choice. Mrs. Gudeese always had a smile and a warm sticky bun, cinnamon roll, or loaf of cinnamon-raisin bread.

Then she died and the store shut down, hollow and empty.

Marion's store would shut down soon, too.

Payton would be forced to move if the council gave the okay to the contractor, hoping the new homes would lure city folk from Denver. What would Hardy do without Payton's shop?

Maybe I should talk to Payton and convince him to move into the old bakery; that way we'd at least keep him in town, where he belonged.

Too many changes.

Hardy pulled into the church's driveway, lifting a hand in greeting to Pastor Haudaire, a good man of God in the small town for as far back as I could remember. Probably hovering around his fiftieth anniversary of preaching.

"How old you think Pastor is?"

Hardy turned off the car and smothered a belch. His bottom lip pooched out. "Forty-eight, forty-nine years he's been here. Probably sixty-nine or thereabouts."

Something inside me deflated at the news. That meant the pastor, who looked so very old, was only about twelve years older than me. I swung the door wide, braced my hand along the roof of the car, and aimed my feet toward the pavement. Hardy hauled me out and up onto my feet.

"You'd think with all this walking I'm doing, I'd lose weight."

"You weighted yourself lately?"

"Weighed, not weighted, and no, the scale and I aren't on speaking terms."

"It told you the truth, did it?"

I drilled him with my eyes. "You'd better shut your trap before I yank them britches up so high you'll sing with the angels."

His eyes glittered. "I sing with angels all the time, next to you in church."

"Oh, you's a sweet talker when you want to be."

He slammed the door. "A smart man knows when to wag his tongue in the honeypot."

I winced as Hardy greeted the pastor with a hearty slap on the back, even though the elderly man seemed frail as glass. I shook Pastor's hand and moved into the sanctuary, where Mark and Valorie sat together on the last pew.

Up front, the organist practiced a slow, mournful

song. No choir to sing for Marion, I noticed, but then, some people didn't want a whole group singing at their funeral.

By the looks of Valorie, she hadn't done much else but cry. I settled myself beside the girl and pulled her into a hug.

Tears sprang to my eyes, and I didn't know if they were sympathy tears for Valorie or genuine tears of grief for Marion. Maybe tears for myself. "Let's get this crying done so's I can rehearse."

Hardy waited until the organist finished and proceeded to the front, where he sat down at the piano and ran through a few small pieces he always used when "getting limber," as he called it.

As I held Valorie, Mark went to the front to lean on the glossy mahogany piano to listen. Hardy never disappointed his listeners. After being married to him for so long, listening over and over to the hundreds of songs he could play or pick out, or even create, I could sometimes still be surprised by the immensity of his gift. He began "Amazing Grace." At first he added a jazz feel to the notes; then it mellowed and softened into a flowing river of promise to the listener. His hands crossed over the keyboard, then down again, and the notes floated my way and wrapped me in the blanket of their mercy.

Emotions spilled through me until the tears came anew, and when I could stand it no longer, I released them. My voice, a soft, low rumble, built with the intensity of Hardy's playing until everything slipped away and I imagined heaven opening its doors and ushering me in. A great longing welled as I held that last note, and my mind came back to the reality of the cold, hard world and the newness of death experienced by the young woman lying like a child against my breast.

Valorie lifted her head and nodded. "My mother always said no one could sing like LaTisha Barnhart. Thank you. That was. . .terrific."

The spell melted completely as Mark laid a hand on Hardy's back and bent to say something. Even from the back, I could see Hardy's pleasure and sense his exhaustion. A good exhaustion.

As we headed back through town to fetch Chief Conrad, silver light cast from the streetlights lit up the front of the various businesses along Gold Street. Your Goose Is Cooked was pitch-black inside, the grocery the only store with any lights on. Tomorrow I'd have to call Mark and explain my reason for not showing up to hash out the new, improved menu I wanted.

"Guess from the lights shining so bright that Shiny's got some customers, even at this time of the evening," I observed as we passed the store.

"You going by Regina's tonight?" Hardy asked.

"Wouldn't hurt none. Then we can go to Marion's and look for the diary. When Mark and I were looking over the books, I saw quite a few."

Hardy's brows pinched together. "I think you're right. That diary could be the key to everything."

As he pulled into the parking space at the station, Hardy slunk down in his seat. "You all gonna make me go with you?"

"You'd miss the chance to go squirreling around in a dead woman's shop?" I teased him.

He shuddered. "Makes me weak to think about it."

"You go on home, then. The last thing we need is you swoonin'."

"I can't believe you're going there tonight. You crazy, woman."

"We've got to find that diary."

He pressed his lips together and shook his head. "You thinkin' Marion had it? Did it ever occur to you she might have been baitin' Dana into thinking that just to get her goat?"

"We'll find out."

Chief appeared after a few minutes. He held the door for me as I got in his police car. I gave a wave to Hardy. He shook his head at me and did a little index finger circle around his ear. He backed out and pointed Lou toward home, leaving me no way to bow out of revisiting Out of Time.

We stopped at Regina's first. The front door opened easily. A pile of mail lay scattered across the floor from where the mailman slipped it through the slot on the door. Chief knelt to pick it up, stacked it nice and neat, and took it with us to the back room where Regina's appointment book lay open on the desk. Chief tossed the stack of mail beside the book, gave Regina's appointments a once-over, though I wasn't sure what exactly he was looking for, then nodded at me. I slapped the book shut. The draft of air blew the mail onto the floor.

Chief grunted at me. I grinned. He bent and scooped it into a pile and froze. I followed his stare to the envelope on top.

"Hmm. Mighty suspicious looking," I whispered.

The writing, plain block letters spelling out Regina's name, plus the absence of a stamp, postmark, or return address, made my mind start ticking. I watched as Chief turned it over. The flap had been tucked in and not sealed. Using the tips of his fingers, chief pulled the paper out. What I saw set my mind on fire.

The sender used block letters on the note inside, too.

Regina,
Marion might be gone, but your little secret remains safe with me. Dead people can't talk. I can. Four hundred by tomorrow noon. Set it on your back step in a shopping bag.

Chief folded the note with great care. "This must have been put through the slot today since we found it with the rest of the mail."

"Or maybe it was already in here on this table and fell when the mail went sailing all over the floor."

Chief moved his fingers to the edge of the envelope. "Let's get this back to the station. I'll call in Nelson and have him run fingerprints immediately."

After we dropped off the envelope and Nelson arrived looking groggy and disheveled, we left again. Within minutes we pulled into a space in front of Payton's music store. A light shone from the back of the store just as it had the night Hardy and I had done our spying.

Chief cut his headlights, but I figured it was too late. If anyone had been in the store, they would have seen the pop of headlights sweep along the interior. As my eyes adjusted to the darkness, I kept my gaze on the place where the light had shone. It still glowed.

Before I knew it, Chief swung the car door open and began to slide from the car. "Whoever is in there will either lay low or try to get away without being seen. I'm going to have a look. I can let you into Marion's and you can start—"

"This woman ain't settin' her bunions into Marion's shop until you get back. I'm no fool."

His smile seemed a bit too condescending. "Afraid of ghosts?"

"No," I snorted. "I'm just not interested in being in there without the light of day and remembering what she looked like the day I found her."

"Stay here, then. I'll be back." He took off at a quick trot, stopped in front of Payton's shop, and cupped his hands on the glass to look inside. He took off again and dropped out of sight around the end of the building.

I relaxed back in my seat and let my mind wander where it would. My run-in with Marion that final day when I quit. . .was fired. . .whatever. . .fanned the flames of my aggravation with her. The woman had been next to impossible. No, not next to, but whole-hog impossible. Through and through. All the time. Never satisfied with the way I did anything. I'd finally had enough and told Marion to back off.

"You gonna make me mad, and you don't want to see me mad," I'd warned.

"I need that paperwork done and filed, and you've had three hours to finish," Marion sniped back as she wiped down the length of the piano with a dust rag.

"If you hadn't taken that long lunch break while I had three customers, I wouldn't be so behind. Why don't *you* do the paperwork for once?"

Her eyes had flashed some powerful heat. "I hired you to do it."

"You hired me to help out in the store, not to run it."

Things had escalated from there. Memories I wanted to forget. I shut down the Memory Lane stroll and wondered when Chief would return. I sat up a little straighter, excited at the prospect that he might have caught Payton engaging in an activity that would explain his new relationship with Dana.

I had my hand on the handle to open the door when I heard what sounded like voices. I became stock-still and strained to hear, jabbing at the button for the power windows, frustrated when the windows didn't lower. As quietly as I could, I opened my door a crack.

Whispers drifted toward me, and I turned my head to try to get the direction. I twisted the rearview mirror and saw the shadows of two people across the street near the school playground. One had longish hair; the other, taller, pulled something out of his back pocket. Whatever it was, he handed it over.

They didn't stick around for long, both taking off

in opposite directions; one toward the Grab-N-Go, the other toward town. I hoped it wasn't drugs or something. I'd alert the chief.

As if by mere thought I could conjure his image, Chief reappeared around the end of the building. I got out and met him at the door to Marion's.

"Something strange going on over at the school. Two shadows exchanging something. Lots of whispering."

Chief chuckled. "Can't arrest kids for looking suspicious, but I'll send Nelson to make sure things are in order."

I clamped my mouth shut and didn't bother to pursue that avenue. I'd keep my ears open around the school. Hated to see kids getting into trouble. That's when it occurred to me what a foolish thing I was getting ready to do going back into Marion's this time of night.

I held my breath as Chief fumbled with his keys, half hoping he wouldn't be able to unlock the door.

He looked amused when he motioned me to enter, and I shook my head and motioned him in first.

"There's nothing in here, LaTisha. Just shadows and inventory."

I started forward. "It's them shadows that give me the crawly feelin'." It smelled mustier and dustier than the last time I'd visited. My eyes were drawn toward the counter, and I shivered at the image that exploded in my head. "Let's get to it and get out of here. I'll check this here first bookshelf." Without waiting for help, I squeezed my way past the dining table and pushed it out of the way, thinking again of Mark shoving the table. I began scanning titles. A strong feeling of that déjà vu people are always talking about raised the hair on the back of my neck. I rubbed my arms to soothe the shiver bumps. A breath of cool air stroked my cheek.

At the second, smaller bookcase next to me, Chief searched the titles there. I finished the first row pretty quickly and began on the second shelf. Third book from the left, I caught the word *Diary* and slid it out. Its burgundy cover, plain and worn, showed its age.

"Look here. Found something. This must be it." I flipped through the pages to find a name and came across one on the back cover. "Fiona Rogers? Dana said it was written by one of her relatives. Was her mother a Rogers?"

Chief put out his hand. "Let me see it."

I handed the diary over to him and kept on checking the spines of the remaining books.

"I don't think so." He tossed the diary on the table. "Mark's doing a study on the history of Maple Gap for another article; maybe he'll know. We'd better keep looking."

We worked in silence for another five minutes before Chief found another one. This diary had a goldish-brown leather cover. It cracked open in his hands. He squinted down at the front cover. "Name is blurry. Looks like a Martin Sorenson."

"Add it to the stack."

Before we finished, we'd found three more between us. I stretched my back and rolled my head to work out the kinks from having my head cocked back so far during my search of the uppermost shelf. Chief gathered up the books in his arms, and by unspoken agreement, we headed to the door.

He took the books to the car. I offered to look through them for him. "You haul them into the kitchen for me, and I'll go over them tonight." Saying as much reminded me of my own books, still in Old Lou's trunk after Chief discovered the box on our last visit to Marion's. If I didn't set those boxes on the kitchen table to remind myself, they'd never make it over to the school.

The first thing I noticed as Chief drove down my road was that is all the lights were on in our house, as if Hardy was in the middle of some great party.

"What's that boy thinking having all them lights on?"

"Maybe the thought of going to the shop really did spook him," Chief offered as he piled the books in his arms and used his foot to push his door open.

I didn't think so.

I opened the side door for Chief and told him to deposit the diaries on the table. "You mind getting those other boxes out of Old Lou? I'm sure Hardy forgot all about them."

"Not a problem," he said and headed back outside.

I blinked around the kitchen and noticed the bowl in the sink. Hardy'd been into the ice cream. I declare, I could have the refrigerator groaning with food and he would still eat ice cream.

"Hardy!" I switched off the lights as I went from room to room. "Hardy!"

"I'm on the phone!"

"Well, you get off there quick. I need some help."

"It's Tyrone. Cora's in labor."

Cora's in labor?"

Silence.

I grabbed my broom and began thumping on the ceiling to get his attention. I had no desire to climb the steps just in time for him to hang up. I thumped again. Harder. A dent appeared.

"Hold on!" he finally hollered. "Pick up the phone before you beat another hole."

Why didn't I think of that? Too much stewing in my brain.

When I picked up, the first thing that grabbed me was the excitement in Tyrone's voice. By the sound of the crackling, he must have been on his cell phone. "I really got to go, Pop. Can't use the phone in there, and I want to get back to Cora."

"Wait a minute," I interrupted. "How's my girl doin'?"

But it was too late. Tyrone had clicked off. Hardy's laughter filled my ear. I slammed the phone down, grabbed the broom, and thwacked it upward hard enough to make a hole. The vague sound of his laughter halted abruptly. I hoped he'd laughed his head off.

"You didn't!" he hollered.

I crossed my arms and smiled up at that hole. "I sure did. You've got no business being so ornery. Get down here and tell me everything before I explode."

Hardy's stocking feet made a padding noise against the carpet as he came down the stairs, a grin on his face.

"Just call me Pappy."

"What's going on? She's got a month to go."

"Doctor is going to work on slowing her down. Tyrone was telling me how he came home from the store and saw her straining. He called the doctor real quick and had her to the hospital in minutes." He lifted the cordless still in his hand. "I'm keeping this close."

"So it's probably not going to happen tonight. You remember Shakespeare was early. No use getting tied in knots—they'll get those contractions stopped."

"No matter. They'll keep her for a while." He ran his hand over his hair, a dreamy look in his eyes. "Me. A Pappy!" he said and gave the strangest little choked laugh. "Maybe they'll name the little guy after me."

Hardy's happiness pulled me along, and my irritation with him dissolved. I put my arm around his shoulders and pulled him close. "Grandbabies. Can you believe it? Makes me feel old, though. Don't like that feeling at all."

"Naw," he muffled against my shoulder. "Not old, just entering a different stage in our lives."

"He's gonna call if something happens?"

"He'll call."

I released Hardy and glanced through the doorway at the kitchen table stacked with diaries, then back at Hardy. "You think we should start out?"

He glanced in my direction and shook his head. "Would be a waste if Tyrone calls back and says all is well." He had followed my line of vision. "Say, what you got there?"

"We found more than one diary. We'll have to search them all." True to his word, Chief had brought in the boxes and set them on my kitchen table. Just waiting for me to dive in. Guess Chief had figured he was done for the night and hightailed it home.

"I got to finish the vacuuming," Hardy said. "Too excited now to sit and read."

"Is that why you have all the lights on?"

"Got home and ate so much ice cream, I couldn't sit still, so I dragged out the vacuum."

"You've no business eating all that sugar."

He flashed his tooth at me. "It's what makes me sweet."

I gave him a good once-over and snorted. "You need all the help you can get. Now get, and let me look over these books." Before he got too far away, I reached out and snagged the cordless phone from his hand. He frowned.

I frowned back. "You won't be able to hear over the vacuum if it rings. I will."

"I ain't deaf, woman."

"I don't want to risk it."

Returning to the kitchen, I fanned the diaries out in front of me. My stomach rumbled. Food called. I grunted to my feet, felt the pinch of my shoes, kicked them off, then yanked open the refrigerator door to itemize everything within. I studied the ingredients I had on hand—I really needed to go shopping—and decided on something quick. Garlic chicken. I flicked the switch to turn on the broiler, plopped two chicken breasts on the broiler pan, and covered them with garlic powder, salt, and pepper.

In five minutes, I had sliced mushrooms and onions and begun to sauté them in a splash of olive oil. When they got tender, I added some frozen hash browns. As I stirred, I relaxed bit by bit, the stress of the day sloughing off me like the paper skin of an onion.

The first diary I started with was written in spidery handwriting that was difficult to read. I gave up after the first three pages when the author began writing about the everyday life of a schoolmarm and single woman. My eyes thanked me for the reprieve.

The smell of the chicken permeated the air. I paused long enough to turn it. The hum of the vacuum ceased, and Hardy came into the room, guided by his nose, no doubt.

"You makin' one of my favorites."

"Finish up those potatoes for me while I read through this diary, will you?"

"What do I look like, the maid?"

"Nope. You look like a man who's not going to eat if he don't get to cookin' those potatoes for me."

He pulled the skillet back onto the front burner and adjusted the flame. "Find anything in those?"

"Lot of old writing about life way back when." I set the diary down and heaved a sigh. This wasn't getting me anywhere, and I wasn't even sure how I knew that.

The letter I had found on Dana's end table came back to me. I could see why, for sentimental reasons, the diary would be important to Dana.

Hardy made a racket pulling the chicken out of the oven. I watched as he dumped the chicken on a plate and spooned potatoes on the side, potatoes falling off the spoon and bouncing off the stovetop. He was as sloppy as the person who had shoved Marion was sly. I felt no closer to a solution now than I had two days ago.

Hardy plunked my plate down and sat down with his. "Let's pray and slay."

He recited his typical prayer. Mentally, I added a postscript. *There's something here I'm not seeing, Lord. Open my eyes.*

We split the stack of diaries between us and ate in silence as we read. Page after page after page, until Hardy finally put down the last in his pile. "Maybe the diary isn't a big deal. You bark up the wrong tree and you're gonna waste more time."

"How'm I supposed to know what to look for?"

"You don't, which is why we're going through these. I'm just saying you shouldn't forget other avenues left unexplored." He stood, stretched, and wiggled his fingers. "I'm going to go play the piano. Isn't Payton coming to tune it after the funeral sometime?"

"Supposed to. Wonder if Dana ever got hers in tune."

"We could try it out tomorrow. Give you a chance to ask her about the diary."

And possibly I could find out where she'd gone for those few minutes left unaccounted for on the day Marion died. We'd go over all that after the funeral sometime.

I stuffed the dirty dishes in the dishwasher and

worried over Regina. The girl's love for her mother still touched me. If Marion had been the one blackmailing Regina before, who was taking up. . .

I sucked in a breath. *Betsy Taser!*

Certainty swelled in me. It made perfect sense. Betsy's "Put it on my tab" comment, as if Regina somehow owed her something, coupled with the fact that Betsy would have insider knowledge of the events surrounding the theft of money. I felt *good*.

I punched in the number for Chief Conrad's private residence and waited for him to answer so I could pour all the details in his ear. Plus, he could pay Mrs. Taser a private visit to see if her fingerprints matched the ones on the envelope.

He answered, and I loaded him down with my theory. When I hung up the phone, I felt both relieved and confident that Regina's part in Marion's death had been solved. I could strike her name from my mental list of suspects.

I peeked at the clock. Eleven fifteen. I knew I'd better get to work on the diaries again.

In the background, Hardy played fun little tunes.

When the kids were young, they'd spend hours making up words to the tunes Hardy would concoct. The children got to where they begged their daddy to sit down with them every night and play their little game.

The memory took the edge off my enthusiasm. Funny how a momma raises her babies to be loyal to family; then when they get out on their own, they put that into practice by loving their own family. . .to the exclusion of their own mother and father.

Time for me to realize that all children eventually spin away on their own axis, away from the sun and moon of Momma and Daddy. And that realization didn't hurt nearly as much as it had two days ago. Grandmotherhood would be my future. If Cora had her baby tonight, I'd be in a real pickle, what with singing at the funeral and needing to talk to Dana and let Payton in to tune the piano.

Hardy's playing framed my thoughts as I hung the dish towel over the oven handle and decided to get those boxes prepared to drop off at the school on Monday. It sure would be a relief to have them out of the way and off my mind.

I nudged the big box closer and peered in. Right on top, its cover crinkled and ripped, sat a book with the word *Diary* written in faded gold across the cover. I didn't remember it being there when I'd purchased the neatly stacked books underneath it. My fingers grew warm as I reached in and lifted it out.

I cracked the front cover and read the date and the name of the author, and I knew the search was over. The name matched the one I'd read in that old letter on Dana's end table. Coincidence this was not.

I opened my mouth to yell out to Hardy, then clapped it shut. Something about that tune he was playing. Something familiar. It brought to mind that day in Payton's shop when I'd had this same sensation as Hardy played and the chief asked me his questions. I closed my eyes, trying to capture that elusive connection between this tune and that moment. It scratched at my brain until I thought I'd scream. Maybe Hardy could help.

"Hardy." I yapped his name before rounding the corner into the living room.

He didn't miss a note, but the lack of music in front of him didn't help me know the title of the piece, either.

"What's that you're playing?"

"A tune I composed myself," he said.

"I know that. What's the name of it?"

He did a little flourish on the keys and finally answered, "I call it 'Breezin' Across.' I played it for you last week."

The name didn't push an automatic recall button as I'd hoped it might, but it tied in with Marion's death somehow—I just couldn't put my finger on it.

"Well, I'm going to bed. Got some notes to look over for Tuesday's class before I read through this diary. I'm thinking it's the one we've been looking for. Found it right on top of the other books in that box I bought."

Hardy, lost in his music, simply nodded.

The music followed me up the stairs and floated over me, soothing, as I got ready for bed. I snapped on the light at my side, eyed my notebook from class, and shoved it aside. The diary drew me. In order to get peace, I needed to know for sure this was the one we'd been looking for.

I read through what was obviously a man's chronicle of events. Sentences were written tersely, with little description. After the first four pages, I almost put it aside to study my notes for class, but I read another paragraph, then another, until finally, I found it.

> *I worked on my new project. Took up the old*
> *wood. Easy work. Had to do it at night to*
> *keep it a secret, but tacked a blanket over the*
> *window to keep the light in. I'll start small.*
> *Work my way up from there. People trust me,*
> *and I'm the only assayer around for miles.*

If Jackson Hughes was the same one murdered during Dana's great-grandfather's days as sheriff, I could understand the girl's interest in the diary. Maybe Jackson even told the story of how he robbed the townsmen of their gold.

I fanned the pages, noticing the writings did not go all the way to the end but stopped in the middle. I fanned the pages again, slower, and stopped at a crude drawing that took up two pages. Smudged badly, the picture sported rough lines that imitated the outline of a building with two smaller rectangles, like rooms within rooms. Not understanding exactly what I was looking at, it did occur to me that the map might be one of the reasons Dana found the diary so interesting.

The legend of gold and all that. To top it off, this map, combined with any other facts the assayer's diary provided, could be the very reason Marion wouldn't give it back to Dana. But Marion couldn't read.

I flipped back to the front and continued reading, but the assayer went on to other subjects and my eyes grew too heavy to continue.

As I drifted off to sleep, one question rang in my head. Would Dana Letzburg kill for this diary?

21

Saturday morning, bright and early, the phone rang. Cobwebs clung to my brain until Cora came to mind. I sat bolt upright as the phone rang a second time and nudged Hardy none too gently. "Did Tyrone leave a number?"

"His cell phone, but he can't use it inside the hospital." He rolled toward me, smothering a yawn.

The phone rattled again. We stared at each other for one strained, anxious moment; then I yanked the receiver up, both excited and nervous.

"Hello?"

"LaTisha?"

I blinked hard, not registering the voice. My heart slammed hard and sunk to my toes. *A doctor?* Definitely not Tyrone.

"LaTisha?" Chief Conrad's tenor finally registered a face to match the voice.

"Who else would it be?" I barked, yanking my arm away from Hardy's relentless patting. I shook my head at him, hoping he would understand my silent message and leave me be so I could concentrate on what the chief was saying.

"Sorry, this is Chief Conrad. Something's happened down at Marion's shop. Since you were in there with me the last couple of times, I wanted you to come down and tell me what you think."

"Someone break in?"

"I, uh—" His voice held a note of uncertainty. Like saying anything more might reveal more than he wanted.

Hardy slid up in bed and raised his brows in a silent question.

Chief's voice came through low and deep, as if he had cupped his hand around the receiver so his words wouldn't be overheard. "Yeah, someone broke in."

"I'll be there," I promised.

"Thank you."

I bounced myself to the side of the bed and lunged upright. Hardy's voice trailed over my shoulder.

"Can't you get up without creating a tidal wave for the rest of us?"

"You need to get your sorry self out of that bed anyway. Lots to do before the funeral. I want you to try calling Tyrone and make sure they're okay. Then you can make the phone calls to cancel Regina's appointments."

"I ain't the one who volunteered to do all that."

"Maybe not, but that was Chief on the phone. There's trouble down at Marion's place, and he wants me there. I can't make those calls and get down there, too, so you're gonna have to help." I glared at him. "And what's all that fussin' in my face while I'm on the phone? If it'd been Tyrone, I'd have told you so."

"You weren't talking a blaze like usual, so I thought it must be bad news." He climbed from bed as if he were being slowly poured onto the floor. "This is the thanks I get for staying up most the night reading over that diary."

That brought me up short. "You read the whole diary?"

"Sure did." He stretched again, jaw wide open in a humongous yawn. "Know what I think? I think that there little drawing is what Payton and Dana were looking at the other night."

"You talking foolish. How could they when the diary was in the box in the chief's truck?"

"Maybe she'd made a copy."

It gave me something to think on. "What else did it say?"

"He confesses that he hid the gold under the floorboards in a niche."

"That's all?"

He sent me a look of pure disgust. "You want me to go dig it up for you, too? How'm I supposed to know if that's all? That's all that I read; I can tell you that."

When I glanced at myself in the mirror, I noticed my twists were lookin' mighty sad. Since I had to go straight from Marion's to the funeral, I'd have to do something with my hair, unless I wanted to look like a well-stuffed scarecrow as I sang.

"You get Regina's cell phone number the other night?"

"Yeah." He pointed at the pair of pants hung over the chair.

It took me a minute to locate the piece of paper and make the call. No answer. I decided to call the home and see if I could get Regina that way.

"Yes, I'm calling to talk to Regina Rogane, daughter of Eloise Rogane."

The nurse took her time responding, and a bunch of whispering voices in the background made me wonder what was so secretive. "Mrs. Rogane is still not doing well. Eloise's nurse reported that Regina left early yesterday evening. If you see her, could you please send her back? Her mother has been asking for her."

I think I said good-bye. The shock of knowing Regina had left right after we'd dropped her off. . . The obvious questions flooded my mind. I knew if I sat and pondered for too long, I'd be late for everything the entire day. Best to think on my feet.

First, the problem of my hair had to be solved. I typed *twist-outs* in the search engine on the Internet and got directions I could follow. When I took out all the twists Regina had so carefully put in, my hair looked lovely, though I had to do some greasing of the ends a bit to get them tamed and not so fuzzy. After all these years of relaxing my hair, I couldn't have been more pleased at the simplicity of the style.

By the time I emerged from the bathroom, Hardy had regressed back to the horizontal position. Instead of wasting time on him, I planned a new attack.

I dressed hurriedly, pulling on a favorite suit. The skirt seemed not quite so snug. Exercise was doing me some good. I decided I'd put the jacket in Lou until I needed it right before the service started.

A mountain of laundry reminded me I needed to run the washing machine soon. It's not just death and taxes that are a sure thing. Laundry is, too. No time now, though. I skimmed down the steps, remembered something I'd wanted to tell Hardy, grabbed the broom handle, and whacked on the ceiling until I heard him moaning and muttering about something. Probably the new dents in the ceiling.

"And don't forget to check on Tyrone and Cora!" I yelled up at him.

He yelled back with some type of gibberish that I didn't bother to translate as I propped Regina's appointment book against a glass of just-poured OJ. Sliced grapefruit and a bowl of cereal, all arranged on the table along with an "I love you" note, would hopefully be the peace offering I needed.

I checked the clock and started for the door when I felt it, the slight release of pressure running a path up my leg. A hole in my nylons. Already. Overnight, my chafed skin, relieved from friction, had soothed a bit, but walking around all day today with a run on my inside thigh. . . I hated the thought of waddling to the front of the church, bowlegged, for all the town to see, then trying to sing "Amazing Grace" with dignity and reverence—that was so not going to happen. I made the mad dash upstairs.

Hardy stood with one leg in his pants, balancing himself against our footboard. He glanced up in surprise and stared, his expression fading into a smile of satisfaction. "You look good. No hat. I like it."

My hair. I'd forgotten. I leaned in and pecked his cheek.

As much as I appreciated the compliment, I had no time to spare. I grabbed a box of new hose and began tugging them and stretching them before maneuvering them into place. And that was my aerobic workout for the day.

—

Chief Conrad met me as I pulled up in front of Marion's. I noticed Payton standing in the window of his store busily dusting a display of CDs and music, alongside an armchair and an occasional table with a flute across the surface, as if the instrument awaited its owner to come and blow sweet music.

Conrad's eyes sparked as I neared. He gave an almost imperceptible shake of his head. I caught on to his unspoken warning against saying anything out loud and followed him into Marion's.

What a sight! Books were strewn around the room as if a terrible storm had blown through, lifting and throwing everything less than ten pounds.

Chief shut the door behind us. "State police are on their way. They think it's directly related to the crime. Don't touch anything."

A lone book, upside down, pages ripped out and scattered, lay on the floor five feet in front of the counter. Another lay spine up on the counter, its cover bent at a right angle. "Someone was really unhappy."

"What's your full impression?"

That was easy. "Just by the condition of the books, I'd say someone either was looking for something specific and didn't find it, then took it out on the books, or this whole thing was staged."

Chief beamed at me. "My impression as well. The lock was broken, so the perpetrator entered through the front door."

I turned to him, gears churning. "Someone is trying to lead us along a path." My heart sank with the weight of my suspicions. "I had to get Regina's cell number, so I called her mother's home. The nurse reported that Regina wasn't there last night."

Chief frowned and ran a hand down his cheek. And then I felt it. I raised my face into the air and sniffed like a bloodhound. Ice ran through my veins. Chief opened his mouth as if to speak, but I stopped him with an upraised hand.

The draft flowed over me again. Old air. Hardy's song title, "Breezin' Along." Everything clicked into place.

"You find something?" Chief's voice probed.

I didn't offer an answer, caressing every surface with my gaze, every crevice. I lost the feel of the breeze as I walked closer to the counter, so I reversed my direction to the middle of the room, and I felt it again. A memory of Mark's casual lean against the dining room table drew me toward the bookcase.

Emptied of its contents, the bookcase appeared forlorn. Another waft of air. I examined the cracks, hearing Chief Conrad's near-silent footsteps behind me. I refused to be distracted and ran my fingers along the line where the bookcase recessed slightly into the wall behind it.

Nothing.

I repeated the process on the other side, and immediately my fingers felt a strong burst of cool air. I stepped back.

"Find something?" Chief whispered.

"There's a draft." I rolled my eyes to him. "You feel it?"

He straightened, eyes studying the breadth and height of the bookcase. "Can't say that I do."

I indicated the place where my fingers had touched the chill air. "Feel this."

His fingers smoothed down the seam, his face grave one moment, melting into a look of wonder the next. "Yes, I feel it now."

"We need to try and move this thing. This could be blocking another room." What I didn't tell him about was the drawing in the diary. Lines that had blurred as I glanced over them last night took on new meaning. Smaller rectangles within one large one.

Working from the side projecting the draft, I tried to get a good hold on the case while the chief skidded the dining table away, allowing us more space in which to work. Beneath our combined coaxing, the bookcase budged an inch. Conrad saw the progress, and we tried again, sliding the bookcase from its position in increments until a five-inch gap of progress appeared. From there, the bookcase swung inward quite easily.

A dark, narrow space beyond beckoned us. I held my breath as I wedged myself through the opening into the long, very narrow room. Cold, stale air assaulted us.

Chief stared into the darkness, his whisper both hollow and overloud. "I don't believe this. Do you think Marion knew?"

I made my voice little more than a hiss. "She was always grouching about the cramped shop and its lack of storage. If she'd known of this, she would have used it."

"We need to get a light in here." He took one step farther into the room. My eyes, having adjusted to the lack of light, could make out Chief's outline as he crouched beside something small and, by the glint of it, metal. "A flashlight," he murmured, hefting the thing in his hand. "I guess we're not the only ones who know about this little secret."

22

I left Chief to secure the room and went over to the church. The overpowering scent of flowers, mainly those huge mums that seemed the norm for every funeral arrangement, hit me right in the nose. Hardy's nose twitched. I braced myself for one of his sneezing fits, but he rubbed at his nose with a handkerchief and seemed fine.

I relaxed when I saw the closed casket. Valorie must have had a private good-bye earlier. Hardy and I walked down the aisle toward her where she sat next to Mark. Despite Marion's less-than-ideal personality, a good crowd showed. After all, despite everything, she was one of us.

Little Sara waved at me as I passed. I beamed sunshine down on her. Skinny little thing—I'd have to be cooking for her again. Before I had a chance to worry over that, my eyes ran over someone I didn't expect to see. Regina sat right behind Sara, looking fresh and relaxed in a navy blue blouse with white trim. I wanted so much to sit down beside her and ask where she'd been last night.

Last night. . .

Hardy poked me in the back, urging me to move along the aisle. I did, one foot in front of the other, trying to talk myself out of the idea that Regina would be involved in destroying Marion's shop. No time for heading down that rabbit trail now, though. I had a girl to love on.

Valorie's friends sat behind her. Marie. Thelmina—if you can believe that name. Cindy and Mindy—twins. Bobby Walker. Justin Fillmore. They all greeted me and Hardy. These kids, with the exception of the twins, were homegrown. Valorie spilled into my arms the minute she laid eyes on me.

From over her shoulder, Mark's expression showed his concern. He got to his feet and spread his hand over Valorie's back. I understood his agony. Any parent would. To stand by and watch your child suffer is a terrible thing; it rips your heart out and makes you feel bruised all over.

"Will you sit with me?" she whispered into my neck.

"Sure, baby. Why don't you sit down? I think Pastor is getting ready to begin."

I kept my arm around her back as she took her seat. She leaned against me the entire time Pastor spoke about Marion's contributions to the neighborhood and the legacy she left behind. When it came time for me to sing, Pastor nodded my way. Hardy and I went to the front and up the steps. I scanned the crowd, noticing for the first time Payton, dressed in black, a walking silhouette of his normal color choice. His upper body vibrated a bit. I think his leg must have been bouncing, but I couldn't see. He didn't look happy, but, hey, we were at a funeral. When he caught my stare, his eyes flitted aside. I followed his gaze to another familiar figure sitting at the end of the pew in back of him. Dana.

No time to ponder more with Hardy's music building. I zeroed in on Valorie, letting her know with my eyes that this song was for her. Pinpointing one person always helps settle me when a crowd is watching.

Hardy continued to weave a musical spell that floated out over the audience like a cloud and a promise. This amazing grace, his playing seemed to say, is yours for the asking. I lifted my head and closed my eyes and waited. When the music slowed, I slid onto the velvet rainbow of the words and imagined that rainbow wrapping itself around Valorie. Around Mark.

Around each one present.

After the service, I didn't need to make a jump for Regina; Chief Conrad corralled her into a corner as soon as Pastor finished his prayer. He'd milk her for the truth. I hoped.

Hardy made a beeline for who knows what. I lost track of him in the jumble of bodies swarming the aisle. My attention went to Valorie. Mark helped her up, and they headed toward a side door that Pastor Haudaire held open for them. His private office.

When Mark turned in my direction, his expression appeared a little desperate. I took the cue—men are so clueless in the face of emotion—and followed them into the private study and planted myself on the rich, burgundy leather sofa. It smelled wonderful and felt buttery soft. Mark sat in an armchair across the room, his eyes on Valorie, slumped on the sofa next to me, still sniffling and wiping her nose with a wad of tissues.

Pastor whispered something in Mark's ear, received a nod in response, and left the room, closing the door softly behind him.

"Pastor's going to get us some coffee and donuts. We didn't want a big meal or anything, so he said it's the least he can do."

I'd wondered about that. No food after the funeral. But with Marion not having anyone other than Valorie, I supposed it made sense. I would rustle up something later and take it over to Mark's place for the two of them.

Valorie leaned her head on me. I stroked her hair. "It's okay to miss your momma."

"I just wish I'd had the chance to say a proper good-bye."

There it was again, that zing along the edge of my mind that told me this girl had more than grief on her mind. It wasn't just my curiosity making me want to hear what she had to say. She needed to get it out of her system. "You want to talk about it?"

Valorie squelched a sob and buried her face in my arm. I glanced over at Mark, thinking maybe he knew about what was troubling the girl. His jaw firmed, and he lowered his gaze.

Alarm bells screamed in my head. He knew.

"We had a fight." Valorie pushed back a little, dabbing at her eyes. "A huge, terrible fight." Her lower lip trembled hard. "I told her I hated her." She broke down again into gut-wrenching sobs. But I knew her confession would also bring healing. At least, I prayed that way.

Mark crossed an ankle over his knee and jiggled his foot. "We all said some pretty terrible things."

"You were there?"

He nodded, looking miserable. "I told her I wasn't keeping the secret any longer, that I wanted to be a part of Valorie's life, not just a nice stranger. I told her I had DNA tests to prove everything, should she lie and say I wasn't Valorie's father."

Valorie calmed in my arms, her slender body melting completely against me. "I told her I wanted him in my life."

That hatched a question in my brain. "So when did you find out he was your daddy?"

Mark answered for Valorie. "I told her about a week ago."

"Mom didn't know that I knew he was my dad. She knew we were friends. I told her the night before—" She gulped then covered her face with her hands.

"Mmm." I could imagine Marion blowing her stack. "I'm sure that didn't set well with her."

"She ranted and raged and began taking everything out on Valorie," Mark said. "Telling Valorie how her cheating brought such shame, that she'd never amount to anything if she listened to me."

"I was so mad, Mrs. Barnhart." She sucked back another sob. "I was afraid to say anything, but it kept eating at me—"

"Both of us would do things differently if we had the chance. But we won't, and that's part of what we have to deal with," Mark said, staring at his jittering foot.

I wondered if he realized how this looked.

Their confession had the ring of truth. A knock on the office door signaled the return of the pastor. I shot Mark a look. "It would be good for you both to talk to him. Forgiving others can be a lot easier than forgiving ourselves."

What I really wanted to do was ask Mark my questions about the break-in at Marion's. I doubted Chief had a chance to mention it to him, in light of the funeral. I sighed. Valorie didn't need anything else to rock her world right now. I'd have to hold off.

A little smile curved Valorie's lips as she sat up. "Thanks."

I patted her cheek. "Deep down, you know your momma loved you, Valorie. Very much. She just had a problem showing it sometimes." As I spoke, my mind went to my reaction to Shayna. "We mommas love so strong that we have a hard time knowing when to let go."

Pastor set a box of donuts on the table by Valorie and peeled off the lids of a coffee and a hot chocolate. I heaved myself to my feet and served Mark a look.

I'd never seen him look so. . .so. . .humble. He and I shared a long, silent stare before Pastor Haudaire blocked him from view as he offered Mark the coffee.

"Pastor, I—I think it would be good if my daughter and I talked to you."

I made my exit right then, knowing I'd left them in good hands. They'd made the first step; the rest wouldn't be quite so hard.

Not one person remained in the sanctuary, so I beat it out of there. In the parking area, Dana stood talking to Sara's mother, while Sara clutched her mother's hand and stared at Dana. When she saw me, she broke free and ran over.

"Hey, little gal." I greeted her with a hug.

"Mommy and Dana are talking about clothes."

I matched her smaller steps but kept on course to the car, where I could see Hardy sitting, drumming his fingers on the steering wheel. I glanced at my watch. Payton would be at our house in a little less than an hour.

"I was getting bored."

"Talking about clothes?" I tried to look exasperated. "How can you call yourself a girl when you get bored talking about clothes?"

She giggled as if I'd said the funniest thing in the world. "I told Ms. Letzburg she looks as pretty today as she did the day I saw her going into that dead lady's shop. She said thank you, and Mom asked her where she got her outfit."

I ground to a halt. Sara grinned up at me, unaware of the maelstrom she had loosed. I took her hand and tugged on her piggytail, not wanting to appear abrupt or scare her, but I knew the next few minutes were important.

"You saw Ms. Letzburg the other day? I thought you was in school."

"I was in school. We have recess before lunch. Mary and me played hopscotch, and I won. She got mad at me and left."

"Ms. Letzburg play with you then?"

Sara giggled. "No, silly. She was all dressed up like she is today walking down the sidewalk. I waved at her, but she didn't see me and went into the dead woman's store."

Excitement buzzed around inside my body. But I needed to get an idea of the day and time.

"You sure it was Ms. Letzburg?"

Sara's head bobbed in the affirmative. "She has on the same outfit as she did then."

No way to find out what I needed to know but to come right out and ask, though I hated to do that for fear Sara might go back and let it slip to Dana that I'd been pumping her for information. I had to try. I massaged my brain. Then I got an idea.

"I hope you ate all your lunch that day."

She scrunched up her nose. "No. They had carrots and meat loaf. Yuck."

"Sara!" Her mother called out from the other side of the parking lot. Sara gave me a quick hug before she skipped away.

"Love you, sweetie," I called after her, my eyes on Dana as she slid into her car. At least I didn't have to worry about Sara letting it slip that we'd been talking about her.

23

"I got us a date over at Dana's this afternoon," Hardy informed me as soon as I set foot in the car. I blinked at him and yanked the safety belt around me, my brain in a buzz.

His hand on my arm tugged me around to what he'd been flapping his lips about. "You lookin' a little splotchy in the face. You have indigestion again?"

"No, I don't have indigestion. Sara told me she saw Dana one afternoon last week walk into"—I made air quotes—"'that dead woman's shop.' What you think of that?"

"What day? It's been locked up tight."

"Whatever day they had meat loaf and carrots on their menu at the school. I'll have to call Wilma Billings. She's head cook."

"Shouldn't be hard to find out," he said as he slipped the car into drive and we chugged out of the parking lot.

"You talk to Payton about anything else?"

"Maybe." He pointed a finger at a toothpick stuck in the seam where the fabric on the roof met the plastic of the side. "Hand me that thing."

I snorted. "You've only got one tooth to pick— why you need it?"

"Like to suck on them." He pulled a face. "And I've got plenty of teeth in my head yet."

I handed it over, trying to hide my irritation at his

change in subject. Sometimes it just wasn't worth it for me to admit he knew something I didn't. He knew how it irked me when he savored a juicy tidbit I had no knowledge of. "You'd better stop playing your games with me, Hardy Barnhart."

He gave me a cheeky grin, the toothpick stuck to his lower lip. "Payton didn't talk much."

I waited for him to continue, but when I looked over at him, his mouth worked the toothpick instead of forming more words. "And. . . ?"

"Don't get your stockings in a twist. I'm just messin' with you. But you think on it a minute. Payton's a nervous chatterer, usually saying something to fill the emptiness, and today he was quiet. Real quiet."

Ah. I saw where he was headed. Maybe. "It was a funeral. He's probably being respectful."

"Could be," he conceded, pulling the car into our driveway. "I did call and talk to Tyrone. Cora's doing fine. They sent her home to rest. I told him we'd check on them tomorrow."

The news of Cora relieved me. With that worry laid low, I could turn my complete attention to this mystery. I wanted so badly to figure out this whole thing. I trusted Hardy's observation of Payton, his being the man's friend and all.

Inside the house, I let my purse fall to the table and picked up the phone first thing to dial Wilma. It took her a minute to lay her hand on a menu, but when she did, I felt my scalp tingle at the news. I hung up fast.

Hardy's rear end stuck out of the refrigerator as he

dug around. "Sounds like good news," he muttered.

"It is. Sara, bless that baby's heart, is gonna get a whole pie for this."

He backed out of the fridge, clutching lunch meat in one hand, the jar of mayonnaise in the other. "Do I get a whole pie? Blueberry?"

I gave him a caustic look and grabbed the sandwich makings out of his hands. "Give me that! You eat more than any man I know."

"And I burn it all. What you flappin' at me for?" He struck a pose. "You just can't stand my fine physique."

Laughter bubbled. He looked like a plucked chicken standing there, biceps the size of an egg, acting as if he were some Greek god. "Oh, I can stand you all right. I'll stand you right outside this door and not let you in until I'm through with my thinking."

Hardy's eyes crinkled at the corners, and he hitched his britches up high to rankle me. "I expect I'll be outside a long while, then."

I slapped the mayo and cold cuts down and lunged for him. He hightailed it outside, not even shutting the door. Honestly, he needed a good ear-wringing. He sure was a pert little thing. But as much as we pecked at each other, I knew I'd never want to nest with any other man.

I threw together a sandwich and yelled out the door for him. He was hanging over the fence talking to our neighbor. Since I needed to do some cooking for Valorie and Sara, I started banging around in my pots and pans drawer.

My thinking session began with chopping onions and a green pepper, then rolling ground beef into balls and browning them on the stove. The more my mind spun around the events of the morning, the more I came back to Mark and that dining table. In light of the secret room, it seemed way too coincidental to think he'd done it accidentally. If he knew about the room behind the bookcase, why didn't he tell Chief?

What was he hoping to do by butting the dining table up against it? The flashlight we'd found didn't work, and we were forced to leave so we wouldn't be late for Marion's funeral.

Hardy's voice boomed out a greeting, and I heard a car door slam. It was too early for Payton. I stirred together tomatoes and minced garlic before wiping my hands and peering out the side door. Chief Conrad's face framed in the glass about made me jump out of my girdle. I shot back and heard his laugh.

"You spying on me now?" he asked as he slipped inside.

"What are you doing, trying to scare me dead?"

"No, sorry." He chuckled. "I came by to tell you that Regina came back because she had to pay that money and knew it was due this afternoon. She confirmed it was Betsy picking up where Marion left off, but I'm processing Betsy's fingerprints and trying for a match before I proceed. I knew you'd want to know."

Hardy slipped in the door. Never shy about eating in front of others, he started right in on his sandwich, but I knew he had his ear cocked toward our conversation.

I told Chief about Sara seeing Dana go into Marion's Tuesday at around eleven o'clock. We swapped theories about the purpose of the secret room when Hardy interrupted.

"I can tell you what that room is. It was the assayer's office. He says so right in the diary. That little map shows the layout of the building. He was trying to think of a good hiding place for the gold and must have doodled that map."

Chief and I stared at Hardy in stunned amazement.

"You knew about the room?" Chief asked.

"He read the diary all the way through last night," I said, answering the question.

"Yeah, and if you had read it all, too, you would have known." Hardy paused to wipe at a smear of mayo on his lip with the back of his hand. "He tells you pretty plain about his little operation."

Chief pivoted toward the door. "I'm going over there right now, with a good flashlight, and having another look around that room."

24

Someone was looking for the diary.

That's the only conclusion I could settle on as I finished up the pot of spaghetti and turned it low to let it simmer. It was the only explanation for Marion's bookshop being ransacked.

Deciding I'd better have another look, I brought the diary down from upstairs and settled with it into a cozy armchair in the living room. The front window looked out over the driveway, so I'd know Payton was here the moment he arrived. I'd let Payton in, then leave to find Mark. By now he'd know about the break-in at Marion's.

My concentration shattered when I saw Payton's car turn into the driveway. I huffed up from the chair and set the diary aside as Payton and Hardy tumbled in together. Payton had ditched the monochromatic look, and the musician's newest garb screamed so loudly it hurt my eyes to look at him.

"LaTisha! So good to see you again." He held out his hand as he inched closer. "It's been a long time since we've talked. Terrible about Marion."

I rolled my eyes at his extended hand. "Something in that brain of yours is just rattling along. Don't have time for your nonsense; I need to go see Mark. You tune that piano real good now, you hear?" For a nanosecond, I thought I saw his features pinch, but his expression morphed into a show of bright eyes and big teeth. Nice teeth, truth be told.

"Have a nice visit. Send him my best."

Hardy threw his keys up in the air and caught them. "I'll be waiting for ya."

But I wasn't done with Payton. "You'd have more customers come in to look around your store if looking at you didn't hurt so much." I rubbed my eyes to highlight my point.

Payton's smile didn't budge. "Don't like the new threads, huh?"

I laid a bit of bait on a hook. "Wearing those clothes lights up a room so much, you probably won't need electricity. Speaking of which, I saw some lights on in your shop the other night. You're gonna have a whopper electric bill."

His smile flattened the slightest bit. "I must have forgotten."

Hardy broke my questioning as he hollered a warning to me. "Best hurry, woman. I ain't waitin' on you."

Payton opened his bag and began to dig around. I scrammed out of the house and made my way down the driveway, where Hardy waited.

"Let's walk," I suggested.

"You sure?"

"The exercise will do us good." And give me a chance to process Hardy's announcement that the secret room used to be the assayer's. Could be that was the reason Payton rallied for his building to be declared historical. If he truly knew. . . And why shouldn't he? The legend was well known. Dana, too, would have an inside track, being a Letzburg and all.

"How do you think Mark could be involved in this whole thing?"

Hardy matched my pace and swiped his forehead with the back of his hand. His jaw worked back and forth as he mulled on it. Deciding not to push him for an answer, I released my thoughts to the beauty of the day and let the sunshine wash over me. Too much thinking made my head feel all clogged. I breathed in the fresh, clean air. The sun on my skin turned from pleasant to hot in short order, and I quickly recalled why I'd decided to drive this morning. Still, aching feet and all, I needed this time out in the air. Just ahead, we'd be shaded by the arching branches of the trees that lined our road, reducing the heat of the sun to bearable proportions.

We made it all the way to Gold Street before Hardy finally responded.

"He writes that article for the paper. He's doing his own research on Maple Gap. Could be he ran across something that got him to thinking Marion's building was important.

I latched onto that line of thinking like a moth to light. If Mark had Valorie's key to the shop, what would prevent him from entering whenever he liked? Chief hadn't bothered with putting a different lock on the door. Was Mark looking for the diary? But his pushing the dining room table to block the entrance still remained unexplained.

We crossed Gold Street when we came parallel to Your Goose Is Cooked.

The sign in the door read CLOSED.

On the way back home, my legs chafed in step with my temper. Why hadn't I called first and saved myself a trip? Hardy remained quiet. For once. When we turned off Gold Street to Spender Avenue, I glanced down the road, gratified to see Chief's car outside Marion's. Maybe this wouldn't be a wasted trip after all.

"Let's go see what Chief's up to."

Through the window, I could see only the shadowy outlines of furniture. Hardy tried the door and I hollered out, not wanting to startle the man.

Chief poked his head out of the hole in the wall. "Guess what I found?"

"A skeleton," Hardy guessed as a shudder ran over his body.

"Nope."

My turn to guess. "A dead body?"

Chief laughed and pointed a finger. "You've been reading too many criminal science textbooks."

I waited for Chief's explanation. His gaze went to Hardy, a tiny smile playing about his lips. The moment the lightbulb went on in Hardy's head, I could see the bright light shine from his eyes. Too bad I was clueless. Chief smiled huge. "Yup, Hardy. That's right."

Now, you can guarantee I didn't like this non-talk talk one bit. Something brewed between these two men, and they were enjoying it at my expense. I crossed my arms. "I'm gonna be bangin' some heads in a minute, *po*-lice officer or no."

Chief busted out laughing. Hardy joined in.

The nerve!

I reached out a hand and gave Hardy's drawers a good upward yank. He shut up. His eyes got buggy.

Chief might have choked to death trying not to laugh if I hadn't narrowed my eyes in his direction. "Talk. And make it quick."

He sobered up nicely as Hardy worked on getting his britches lowered a notch. "Nothing really, LaTisha. I figured since Hardy worked out the drawing in the diary so well. . . Anyway, we found a partially boarded-up entrance that leads right up to the back of one of those uprights Payton was moving around the day of Marion's death."

"He's at our house right now tuning the piano. Sounds like you'll need to be asking him some questions."

Chief rubbed his jaw. "I'll get Officer Simpson over here to help me get all those boards off first. Whoever nailed them up must have used an entire box of nails. Then I'll find Payton and ask him a few questions."

I headed for the door, thinking of my simmering sauce and wondering if Payton would be done with the piano yet. I had a few questions of my own.

25

Hardy trotted along beside me in a huff over what I'd done at Marion's. Let him huff. He could puff and blow the house down, too, and I'd say he got what he deserved. Ornery critter.

I tried to adjust my hose by pulling on them through the fabric of my dress so my legs wouldn't rub so badly. They burned like fire. But I hoofed it back to the house in record time. Payton's little subcompact—yellow, if you can stomach the thought of that—glowed in my driveway for all to see and be blinded by.

Satisfied I'd have my say, I went in the side door, gave my sauce a stir, and turned off the burner. Hardy pooched his lip out at me and headed up the steps. I let Hardy pout and headed toward the living room. Payton leaned into the front of the piano as he hit a key and cranked his little tool thingie back and forth.

I took a seat in the armchair I'd been in earlier. "Was over at Dana's the other day. She was complaining that her Steinway didn't sound tuned even after you'd tuned it."

Payton froze, his elbow locked in mid-crank. His posture radiated shock. Ever so slowly he straightened, lowering the tool. He met my gaze.

The pattern of his clothes seemed to gyrate and throb as he plunged his hand into his bag and dug around. In seconds he had gone from a genial piano tuner to a stranger. His movements became jerky, and a line of perspiration broke out on his forehead.

I decided to push further. "You know what else? Chief let it loose that he found a secret room in Marion's store. You know about that?"

"No."

But his answer held definite bite. I had struck a nerve. I feigned acceptance of his answer and got back on my feet, delighted at the obvious distress I'd stirred in the boy. "Well, I'm guessing you don't need me here buzzing around your head. I'll go check my spaghetti sauce."

In the hallway, out of sight of Payton, I allowed myself a smile while forming the questions I would ask in my next attack.

Within minutes, Payton yelled out.

"I'm all done. I'll send you the bill."

Shocked, I set the lid back on the sauce and headed toward the hallway, but the door clicked behind him. *Guess I stirred up more than my sauce.* Though disappointed I'd not been able to ask him any more questions, I knew Chief was waiting for Payton at the other end. In the meantime, Hardy and I would go see Dana.

I found Hardy in the living room going from table to table, moving magazines around, even checking the shelves of my bookcase.

"What you looking for?"

He stopped in the middle of the room, hands on his hips. "Where's the diary?"

"You had it upstairs last night."

"I looked up there."

It came to me in a flash. "Oh!" I pointed at the armchair where I'd sat and talked to Payton. "I brought it down here. Set it there when I saw Payton arrive to—"

Hardy's brown eyes snapped. "I think we got a thief."

I turned on my heel. "We can head over there and get it back."

"No, we can't."

I spun. "And why not?"

He tapped the crystal of his wristwatch. "Because I told Dana we'd be over at her place at three, and it's two forty-five now."

We stared at each other for a full minute, and I knew the time had come for me to lay it out. "I'm sorry."

Hardy shuffled up close. "Me, too. I shouldn't have harassed you. I know how you hate me doing that."

"Truce?"

"If I can have some of that spaghetti sauce."

"We don't have time. I haven't made the noodles."

"Then I get two blueberry pies."

I rubbed my hand over his head. "I can do that."

We bandied the questions we should ask Dana as Hardy hauled us over there in Old Lou. He recommended asking her why she rescinded her report that the diary was stolen if she hadn't found it.

"We're not 100 percent sure this is the diary," I added. But the name on the diary matched the one in the letter, so how could it not be? "I want to know what she was doing at Marion's shop that day."

"Doesn't look like she was delivering a party invitation."

A chill ran through me. "What if Dana actually

was the one who pushed her? If they had a real fight over Valorie's cheating—"

"Don't you worry none." Hardy reached over and rubbed his hand over my knee. "I'll be right there to protect you."

I didn't feel reassured.

26

As we got closer to Dana's house, my eyes took in the townspeople filling up at the Grab-N-Go on the corner. Got an eyeful when I saw the price of gas. But the man standing beside a hunter green sedan really got my heart to pounding with excitement.

I leaned over toward Hardy as the turn signal clicked on and he began the turn. "No, no, go there!" Confused, he tried to straighten the wheel. I grabbed hold and tugged it to the right so he'd pull into the Grab-N-Go.

"What you doin'?"

"Mark. I want to talk to him."

"That's all you had to say. No need to go jerking the wheel."

Granted, but I was so excited to find him and see what he knew about Marion's store. I heaved myself out of the car and slammed the door hard before Hardy even had the car in park. Didn't have to go far, though, because Mark jogged right up to me, a wide grin on his face. Looked more relaxed than I'd seen him in a while. I quickly turned my shoulders away from Mark and dug down to bring out some money, handing it through the window to Hardy.

"I want a drink. Get yourself one, too, but make sure I get the change."

"You gonna make us late."

"Then hurry."

I turned back toward Mark as Hardy went off to complete his mission.

"Your talk with Pastor went well?"

"I came over to thank you for suggesting it, LaTisha. I admit I wasn't real sold on the idea. Valorie's doing a whole lot better, too."

"She'll grow by leaps in the next couple of years."

He leaned against Lou and crossed his ankles. "Guess you heard about the break-in?"

"Heard about it this morning." I zoomed in on his expression, making sure I didn't miss any reaction he might have at my next statement. "Heard, too, that the police thought it looked staged."

The slightest crinkle of amusement played at the corner of one of his eyes, but he remained silent.

I took the plunge. "You know about that room behind the bookcase, don't you?"

Whatever his reaction, I wasn't prepared for him to slap his thigh and let loose with a string of deep laughs.

"You're good, LaTisha. Real good."

Stunned. That's what I was. Absolutely stunned. Was this boy making a confession? Naw. Confessions meant surly looks and the possibility of physical harm to the good guy—me. I narrowed my eyes, very much aware and relieved that the Grab-N-Go provided many witnesses in case Mark got it in his head to bash me. Hardy, too, would be right at my side, as long as he got back with our drinks in time. "You saying you did the breaking in?"

He leaned close enough that I could smell the scent of bubble gum on his breath. "I did it." He held a finger to his lips.

"Whatever for?"

"You know those articles I'm getting ready to run on Maple Gap?"

Aha!

"I put two and two together looking over an old map of the town at the library. Marion wouldn't let me in her store, but after she died, I spent quite a bit of time poking around until I found the bookcase. Good thing for me Chief didn't let the state police lock the place down. But Valorie had no idea that I used her key, and it might upset her if she knew. . ."

I got his meaning.

Hardy hustled up to the car and got in, waving his hand out the driver's side window. "Come on, we gonna be late."

Mark, easy as you please, walked beside me and opened my car door. He hunkered down and spoke through my lowered window. "Just so you know, I have every intention of talking to the chief."

Hardy put the car in reverse, and Lou crept backward. Mark got the message and stood, slapping a hand on the door and waving. "Where you off to now?"

As Hardy maneuvered Lou into drive, I hollered back, "Dana's place."

Funny thing, Mark didn't look too happy about that. I grabbed my drink and took a long pull at the straw, wondering what it meant.

I tapped Hardy on the arm. "Where's my change?"

He grunted, took a hand off the steering wheel,

and passed me a handful of coins and a crumpled dollar bill.

***

Dana greeted us amiably enough. She offered us tea. I declined, remembering my last episode. Hardy accepted. We followed her into the living room. Hardy's eyes fell on the Steinway like a man starved. First off, I noticed the boxes. Where few books had been before, now the shelves were completely bare, as if instead of unpacking, she was packing.

Dana gave a wan smile as Hardy seated himself; then she trotted off toward the kitchen.

I continued my inspection. There were no papers on the end table this time. No end table, either. Only the armchair remained. As if the place had been stripped of everything just before our arrival. Strange. I sauntered toward the dining room expecting to see all the frills stripped away from the furniture. I was wrong. The room turned out to be completely empty. From my spot, I could see straight into the kitchen. Her cupboards, her table. There wasn't anything. Even the door had been stripped of its thick lace curtain.

She moved between the sink and stove, filling a kettle with water and transferring it. With her back to me, I had the advantage of watching her. She paused at the sink, hands braced on the lip, and drew in a deep breath. Then another. She reached up to the cabinet, flicked open the door, and took down two of the four teacups inside. One slipped out of her grip and shattered on the floor. She stared down at it, her hair swinging to cover her profile.

I figured now was a good time to let my presence be known. "You okay, Dana? Need some help?"

She swung toward me looking like a trapped animal. "No. No, I'm okay. I dropped a teacup. I'll. . .get the broom."

"You look like you're packing up. You moving?"

All the color drained from her face. "I decided the dining room furniture was too much. I. . .sold it."

Seemed to me she liked that furniture pretty well, being it was the only room in the house completely set up last time I visited.

She squatted next to the cup and tried to work the broom and the dustpan at the same time. The kettle let out its first warbling whistle, and she jumped, the dustpan tilting at a crazy angle.

I tried to keep my voice light. "Lovely outfit. Is it new? Sara told me you and her mom were talking clothes this afternoon. She wasn't too happy. Said she'd seen you in that outfit before anyway. The same day they served meat loaf at school." I tapped my chin as if thinking. "Tuesday, I think it was."

Dana's eyes darted to my face. I could feel her tense up, trying to gauge my words so she could match her responses. I went cold. Behind her expression, a malevolent force seemed to brew. If I didn't miss my mark, Ms. Dana Letzburg was getting angry.

The whistle of the kettle became steady. I pointed. "Noisy thing."

She pivoted to the stove and tugged the kettle off

the burner. I decided I'd better retreat a bit. "Sounds like Hardy's enjoying your piano."

I escaped through the dining room, imagining I could feel Dana's eyes burning through my back. Something clattered behind me. I kept going, feeling a real urgency to get to Hardy.

When I went over to stand by Hardy, he raised his eyes in silent question. I patted my forehead like I was wiping sweat. He kept on playing while I made comments to him out loud, hoping the chatter would lower Dana's guard. I had pushed too hard.

She finally came into the living room. Her nostrils flared, her expression cold. No teacups or silver service. Hardy caught sight of her and stood up. "Your piano still isn't sounding real good. Maybe old Payton is losing his touch."

"He's had a lot on his mind lately." She leaned against the doorway.

"Yeah, I guess." Hardly paused. "Read in the paper where you'd reported a theft. Was that the diary you and LaTisha talked about?"

"Yes."

"Chief was talking to me and LaTisha about that. He said you said you'd found it. Funny thing." He rubbed his jaw. "When LaTisha brought her boxes inside the other night, we found an old diary on top. You think it's the one you lost? Or maybe it's the one you found?"

"No, it's the one *I* found, Hardy." Payton shouldered his way through the doorway, diary in hand. Dana straightened and moved aside, relief sliding across her face.

My heart pounded hard. Hardy didn't seem the least flustered by Payton's sudden appearance.

"So you did find it." Hardy cracked a grin. "LaTisha declared she laid it down somewhere in the living room, but when she got home, it wasn't anywhere to be found."

Nothing seemed right about this scene. When had Payton arrived? Why hadn't I heard him knock?

"Well, you can give me that there diary back," I said. "Mark will be needing it to see if we can find the gold."

"We?" Payton's smile stuck to his lips, though his eyes held a hint of darkness. "There won't be any *we* in this, LaTisha. There's already been too much already, and we're going to take care of that tonight, with the help of this." He held up the diary. "Then Dana and I are going to slip this town."

So that's what's up with the boxes sitting around. "What if that gold is just a legend?"

Payton's gaze went to Dana. "Then we'll use the little nest egg Dana's been working on."

Selling grades.

"You gonna just leave your music store?" I could tell by Hardy's tone that the thought of those grand pianos being left behind horrified him.

"They'll be picked up by the manufacturer. I'm tired of trying to make ends meet in this loser town." He flexed his right hand. "Maybe the gold will give me a real chance at having my hand fixed to where I can play again." His expression opened up as he smiled at me. "You're pretty smart. You almost caught Dana and me one night. That was the night we found our secret entrance boarded up. I couldn't believe you'd found it so fast."

"I didn't find it until this morning."

Payton's eyes darted toward Dana, then back at me. "Then who?"

But his question seemed suddenly far away as my mind flashed back to that morning I found Marion dead. The shivers on my arms at the draft of air I'd felt. The bookcase. The entrance to the secret room through Payton's store.

Every bit of moisture in my mouth evaporated. Dana had gone to Marion's shop that morning. . . .

Dana's eyes were on me. "I know what you're thinking. I didn't know about the room until Payton told me the night Marion died. I'd called Payton over that evening to get him to retune my piano, but instead he confessed he'd taken the diary."

Payton gave her a hard look. "That's enough. Let her figure it out on her own. We've got to get moving."

Hardy grabbed my hand. "Then we won't be keeping you two another minute."

Payton blocked one side of the doorway, Dana the other. "We can't let you two leave. I came over to show Dana the diary. Figured we'd have to detain you two to give us a chance to look for the gold before you did." He nodded at Dana, and she left her post and headed toward the kitchen.

"Now don't you be foolish, boy," I admonished.

"You know, it always did hurt my feelings that you didn't like my clothes. You should be relieved to know that I'm leaving town."

I heard the opening and closing of some drawers in the kitchen. Hardy squeezed my hand tight, his palm turning sweatier with each passing second. "What did you do to Marion?"

For the first time since he'd arrived, Payton got jittery. His eyes flicked between Hardy and me. He licked his lips. "She fell."

"A simple fall wouldn't kill someone like her."

His lips twitched, and he opened his mouth. "Hurry up, Dana!"

I felt Hardy's hand slide away from mine. "I need to sit down," he murmured.

I turned as he began backing toward the armchair. A quick look at his face, and I knew Hardy would head for the floor any minute. Some help he was gonna be in a tight spot, lying cold on the floor.

When the back of Hardy's knees hit the front of the armchair, he collapsed. I shuffled over to him. With his face tilted toward his lap, he raised his eyes at me. Uh-huh! I got his possum playing scheme. Payton came up beside me, rope in one hand and a roll of duct tape in the other. I needed to create a distraction to give Hardy a chance to make his move. But what?

"Move back, Mrs. Barnhart. I'll tie Hardy up first."

I inflated myself until I stood as tall as Payton, and I knew I was wider. "You ain't tying me up at all. We've got to get him to a hospital." I took a step back and pulled up real hard on the rolled waistband of my hose. Change splattered all over the place.

Payton's eyes went straight to all the coins rolling everywhere on the hardwood. Hardy flew out of the chair and latched onto him like a rabid dog. Dana took a step in their direction and let loose a scream, turned, and ran.

"Tape!" Hardy yelped at me.

I kicked the roll of tape Payton had dropped over toward Hardy, debating in that second whether I should go after Dana or not. She already had a good head start. Instead, I flopped down on Payton. Ripping sounds rent the air as Hardy made short work of wrapping Payton's legs, then his wrists.

"Go after Dana," I told him. "I'll keep him put."

Hardy ran through the doorway, the kitchen door slamming behind him.

Payton, his face turned sideways against the floor and slightly red, muttered unintelligible words beneath the strip of tape on his mouth. I whapped him a good one on his backside and did a little bounce to let him know who was boss. "You keep a civil tongue, boy, or I'll keep it up."

Minutes passed before I heard the front door open and a winded Hardy entered the living room followed by the chief, who escorted a handcuffed Dana, trailed by Mark Hamm.

"How'd you get here so fast?"

Chief answered. "Mark came to get me. Told me all about his breaking in to try and help us find the entrance, and his suspicions about Payton and Dana. I figured we'd better head this way. Good thing, too."

Payton mumbled. I reached down, my hand hovering by the edge of the tape on his mouth. "It's gonna hurt." I yanked it clear.

Payton howled. "Get. . .her. . .off me. I want a. . . lawyer."

Hardy helped me up while Chief knelt to put handcuffs on Payton. I hung on to Hardy real tight.

"Dana's already started talking, Payton," Chief warned Payton as he herded his two prisoners toward the doorway.

"Thanks for sending the chief our way, Mark," I said.

"Not a problem," he replied over his shoulder as he followed the group outside.

"You sure know how to read my mind," Hardy whispered against my shoulder. "Sitting in that chair, I was hoping you'd come up with something to distract Payton long enough to let me have a chance at him."

I rubbed my chin on his grizzled head. "You scared me. Thought you were real sick."

He chuckled. "Was. Started thinking Payton might do something that required my blood. Got a little light-headed. But it cleared when I sat down." His arms tightened around me, and he tilted his face toward mine, eyes glinting. "You okay?"

"Right as rain, babe."

His tooth flashed. "There was one more mystery solved today."

"What's that?"

"Now I know where you keep the change."

Epilogue

The whole story came out in the papers over the course of time. I had a few more details than most but couldn't share them because of my promise to the chief not to let anyone know I'd helped.

Chief filled me in on Payton's confession. I can pass along some of the details for you.

Payton said he'd gone to Dana's to tune her piano. Apparently, Dana chatted nonstop about an old letter from her great-grandfather that verified the diary of Jackson Hughes. Because of mounting gambling debts, Payton felt compelled to find the diary with the intention of getting his hands on the gold. That's why Dana's piano never got fully tuned. After spouting about the letter and diary to Payton, Dana returned to school, giving him the perfect chance to search for, and eventually find, the diary.

Through the night, Payton read the diary and began making a sketch of the map, but a call from one of the guys from the casino interrupted him, and by the time he returned, it was so late he decided to finish the sketch in the morning. But when Chief arrived on his doorstep bright and early, Payton decided his office safe wouldn't be a good place for the diary if the chief returned with a search warrant. In a panic to find a secure, temporary place for the diary, he visited Marion, figuring with all the old books she had in her shop, it would be a good place to hide the diary.

Payton shoved the diary under his coat and walked over to Out of Time. Marion started in on Payton about his rent being late. She finally turned her back long enough for him to slip the diary into a box of books near the counter. The box I had bought that morning.

He wanted to keep an eye on the box in case Marion shifted the books around and he lost track of it, so he intended to get over to Marion's frequently that day. But on his first trip back, he found Marion standing by the counter, the box of books beside her, the diary in her hands.

All Payton could think about was how desperately he needed that diary and the gold. Like anyone would, he assumed Marion had read the diary. He tried to sidetrack Marion. She tucked the diary back into the box on the counter and told Payton I had bought the books. He came around the counter, plucked up the diary, and told her it was his. She got mad and told him that she'd sold it and he couldn't have it. She ordered him to hand over the book. The diary became the object of an all-out tug-of-war. That's when Payton lost it, let go of the diary, and shoved her as hard as he could. He swooped down to get the diary, realized Marion wasn't moving, and then saw the blood.

Shaken to the core, the sound of footsteps on the cement finally pushed him to action. In his shock, he must have dropped the diary, and that's how it came to be in the other box of books I purchased. The box behind the counter on the floor.

Payton beelined for the bookcase and almost made it through when the doorbell alerted him of a customer.

It was Dana. Shaking by now, he must not have shut the bookcase tightly, which is why I felt that draft of air seconds before I discovered Marion's body.

When Chief informed Payton that Marion couldn't read, that her having the diary in her hands meant nothing—other than she might have been able to understand the map—Payton truly broke down.

After he'd calmed down, Chief asked him about Dana. Since she'd seen him at Marion's, Payton knew he needed to appeal to her. When Dana called him the night of Marion's death, angry over her piano still being out of tune and asking what he'd done to Marion, Payton knew she'd seen Marion's body and came right over to buy her silence. The two of them struck a deal to share the gold. A student visited Dana while Payton was there, and he overheard the boy asking for a better grade. At first Payton didn't understand what was going on. Dana shooed the boy off, but Payton understood that Dana had her own little secret business selling grades. It was pure coincidence that he overheard, but enough to secure Dana's silence.

⌒

One conversation that I did get in on was the one between the chief and Mark. We huddled at my house while Mark explained his interest in Marion's shop. Hardy and I took the sofa, Mark and the chief each in armchairs.

Mark went first. "It's as I told LaTisha earlier: I'd studied Maple Gap history and put two and two together to figure out Marion's building probably housed the assayer's office. I borrowed Valorie's key and poked around one night. That's when I found the bookcase and the entrance to Payton's shop. I decided to have some fun with him and boarded up his entrance. Figured to shake him up a bit." He went on to tell chief that he had fought for Marion's building to be declared an historical site mainly to rankle her, but selling it would have also impositioned his business. When Dana started talking about the diary and the possible secret room, it had further fueled his determination to have it declared a historical site until he could find the gold.

With that, the last piece of the puzzle clicked into place in my mind. "The dining room table," I said.

Mark nodded. "I figured Payton would get those boards off eventually. The table was extra insurance on my part that he wouldn't be able to get back into the shop."

"It never occurred to you that Marion's assailant might have used that entrance?" Chief directed the question to Mark.

"Not at first. When it did, I decided to stage the break-in and hope you would find the bookcase and room and investigate Payton a little more closely."

"Why not just come to me instead?" Chief didn't look happy.

"Because I didn't know for sure where the diary was. I'd taken note of all the ones on the bookcase the day you, LaTisha, and I had gone into the store. When those were missing, I thought maybe Payton had taken them."

"You didn't vote about Marion's building," Hardy pointed out.

"Because I knew once my connection to Marion and Valorie came out, it wouldn't look right."

Chief glanced at me. "You have any other questions, LaTisha?"

I turned to Mark. "What about Valorie?"

"I'm taking her away on a long vacation after she graduates."

Indeed, Valorie had blossomed under Mark's care, and though she wouldn't graduate with honors, the school board had decided she could graduate.

But the best news of all to come out of the whole incident was the budding romance between the chief and Regina. I expected once things settled down a bit, Chief would make his feelings known. It would do the town good to have a wedding.

But for now, I can rest my bunions.

S. Dionne Moore is a bunion-free supermom, able to leap piles of homework and loads of laundry in a single bound. Not only does she write, homeschool her daughter, and help her pastor husband, but she plays piano, loves to garden, and encourages other writers.

You may correspond with this author by writing:
S. Dionne Moore
Author Relations
PO Box 721
Uhrichsville, OH 44683

A Letter to Our Readers

Dear Reader:

In order to help us satisfy your quest for more great mystery stories, we would appreciate it if you would take a few minutes to respond to the following questions. We welcome your comments and read each form and letter we receive. When completed, please return to:

Fiction Editor
Heartsong Presents—MYSTERIES!
PO Box 721
Uhrichsville, Ohio 44683

Did you enjoy reading *Murder on the Ol' Bunions* by S. Dionne Moore?

Very much! I would like to see more books like this!
The one thing I particularly enjoyed about this story was:

_____

_____

_____

Moderately. I would have enjoyed it more if:

_____

_____

_____

Are you a member of the HP—MYSTERIES! Book Club?
Yes   No

If no, where did you purchase this book?

_____

Please rate the following elements using a scale of 1 (poor) to 10 (superior):

___ Main character/sleuth   ___ Romance elements

___ Inspirational theme   ___ Secondary characters

___ Setting   ___ Mystery plot

How would you rate the cover design on a scale of 1 (poor) to 5 (superior)? _____

What themes/settings would you like to see in future **Heartsong Presents—MYSTERIES!** selections? _____
_____
_____
_____

Please check your age range:
○ Under 18   ○ 18–24
○ 25–34   ○ 35–45
○ 46–55   ○ Over 55

Name: _____

Occupation: _____

Address: _____

E-mail address: _____